From Slave
to Abolitionist

From Slave to Abolitionist

The Life of William Wells Brown

ADAPTED BY

Lucille Schulberg Warner

FRONTISPIECE BY TOM FEELINGS

Dial Books · New York

Published by Dial Books
A Division of Penguin Books USA Inc.
375 Hudson Street
New York, New York 10014

Library of Congress Cataloging in Publication Data
Warner, Lucille Schulberg. From slave to abolitionist.

Based on The narrative of William W. Brown,
published by the Boston Anti-Slavery Society in 1847.
Bibliography: p.
SUMMARY: Autobiography of William Wells Brown who was born and
raised a slave but when freed, devoted his life to the abolitionist movement.
1. Brown, William Wells, 1815–1884—Juvenile literature. 2. Slavery in
the United States—Personal narratives—Juvenile literature.
3. Slavery in the United States—Missouri—Juvenile literature.
[1. Brown, William Wells, 1815–1884. 2. Slavery in the United States—
Personal narratives. 3. Slavery in the United States—Anti-slavery movements]
I. Brown, William Wells, 1815–1884. Narrative of William W. Brown,
a fugitive slave. II. Title.
E444.B886W37   301.44′93′0924   [B]   [92]   76-2288
ISBN 0-8037-2743-7

For Henry

Adapter's Note

The following pages are based on *Narrative of William W. Brown, a Fugitive Slave,* the slim autobiography, almost an outline, which Brown wrote and the Boston Anti-Slavery Society published in 1847. In subsequent decades as an active abolitionist in the United States and England, Brown elaborated on his life as a slave, a fugitive, and a free man in speeches and writings. To supplement and expand the original narrative, I went to these sources—published lectures, letters, newspaper articles, books, and prefaces to books. When necessary for clarity or continuity, I borrowed and adjusted language from Brown's contemporaries, including Josephine Brown, whose *Biography of an American Bondsman By His Daughter* was published in 1856. I have tried to keep my own words to a minimum.

From Slave
to Abolitionist

One

Autumn 1854. It has been a little more than five years
since I have seen my native land, America. For five years
I have been in the United Kingdom of Queen Victoria.
No person of my complexion can visit this country
without being struck by the distinct difference between
the English and the Americans. The prejudice I have experienced on all and every occasion in the United States—
and, to some degree, aboard the ocean steamer *Canada*—
vanished as soon as I set foot on the soil of Britain.
In America I had been bought and sold as a slave in the

southern states. In the so-called Free States, I had been treated as somebody born inferior: in steamboats, I had to take my meals on the deck; in hotels, to eat in the kitchen; in stagecoaches, to ride on the outside; in trains, to ride in the "Negro car"; in churches, to sit in the "Negro pew."

But as soon as I arrived in England, I was recognized as a man and an equal. The very dogs on the street seemed conscious of my manhood. If my old master appeared here, with the Constitution of the United States in his pocket, the Fugitive Slave Act in one hand and the chains in the other, and claimed me as his property, it would do him no good. I would stand here and look that tyrant in the face and tell him I am his equal.

During these five years, I have traveled over twelve thousand miles and given almost a thousand lectures about the evils of slavery in every town of importance in England, Ireland, Scotland and Wales and have crossed to France on the same mission four times. I have written and published three books, each of which has been received with much attention both here and in America. I have met many famous men. To name only one, I have been a dinner guest at the home of Charles Dickens, the great English writer, who was deeply interested in my abolitionist work, and in me.

England is, indeed, the "land of the free and the home of the brave." But I am anxious to be in America again. I want to return home to battle the monster, slavery. Soon

I will sail back across the Atlantic and travel the length and breadth of the Free States speaking against the atrocities of this system that keeps so many of my countrymen in chains. It is an evil that I understand deeply, for I was born into slavery and lived the life of a slave until I was twenty years old, when I escaped to devote the rest of my days to its abolition.

I was born near Lexington, Kentucky, in 1814. My mother's name was Elizabeth and she had seven children: Solomon, Leander, Benjamin, Joseph, Millford, Elizabeth and me, William. Every one of us had a different father. My father, my mother told me, was George Higgins, a white man who was related to my master and to the Wickliffe family, one of the fine families of Kentucky. As soon as I was born, the man who owned my mother recorded my birth in a ledger that listed all of his property. He owned about forty slaves, twenty-five of them field hands who worked on the land. My mother was a field hand and when I was an infant, she would carry me on her back into the fields and lay me down on the earth. She was whipped by the overseer for leaving work to nurse me—but she often told me later how I laughed with happiness when she came to take me in her arms.

When I was still young, about two years old, my master moved from Kentucky to Missouri and settled into a small town about seventy-five miles up from St. Louis on the Missouri River.

My early life on the plantation was similar to that of most slave children. I ran about freely, had no work to do and was looked after by an old slave woman while my mother was at work in the fields. But at the age of nine, my situation changed.

The wife of my master's brother died, leaving a baby boy who was only a few months old. My mistress took the infant into her house to bring up. When the child became old enough to need a playmate to watch over him, Mrs. Young called all the young slaves together to choose one of us to serve him. We were ordered to run, jump, wrestle, turn somersaults, walk on our hands and go through whatever gymnastic exercises we could think of—and were strong enough to perform. The selection was important both to the mistress, who needed a reliable playmate for the child, and to the slave. Whoever was chosen for the job would become a house servant. He would throw away the skimpy shirt that buttoned around his neck, the only garment any of us wore; the shirt would be replaced by a complete linen suit!

All the slave children joined the contest enthusiastically while the old mistress sat on the porch watching every move we made: fifteen of us, each in his one garment, sometimes standing on our heads with feet in the air—still the lady looked on.

With me, it seemed a matter of life and death for, being closely related to the master, I felt I had more at stake than the others. At last the choice was made. I was told to stand aside and it was an order I obeyed faster than almost any order I have received since then. I was the lucky boy.

That night I was put to soak in a bathtub. Then I was scraped, scrubbed, washed and dried. The next day, the new suit was delivered to the slave quarters. I slipped into it as all the young slaves gathered around. I was the star of the plantation. My mother, one of the best of all mothers, put her hands on my head.

"I knowed you were born for good luck," she said with tears in her eyes. "A fortuneteller told me so when you were a baby laying in your little sugar trough. Go up to the great house where you belong."

With this blessing, I said good-bye to the log hut and the dirt floor and went to the "big house." My mistress received me and immediately laid down the law for my future:

"I give you your young master," she said. "If you let him hurt himself, I'll pull your ears. If he wants anything and you don't give it to him, I'll pull your ears. When he goes to sleep, if you let him wake before it is time, I'll pull your ears."

And she kept her promise. My ears felt the pinch of her tender fingers and gold rings almost every day, and sometimes almost every hour.

Since the young master's name was William, the same as mine, they changed my name to Sanford even though I was almost ten years old.

My fair complexion was a great obstacle to my happiness with both whites and blacks in and about the great house. Strangers often mistook me for a white boy, which annoyed my mistress very much. Once a visitor came to the house when Dr. Young was away. While Mrs. Young was entertaining him, I went through the room. As I passed the major (for he was a military man), he put his hand out and said, "How do you do, bub?" Turning to my mistress, he said, "Madam, I would have known he was the doctor's son even if I had met him as far away as California. He looks very much like his papa."

The mistress ordered me out of the room, saying that I was one of the servants. The major begged pardon for the mistake. After he had left, I was flogged for his blunder!

My master was a doctor, and he practiced medicine in the river town but he also ran a flour mill, kept a store and owned a farm. A finer situation for a farm could not have been found in the entire state. The climate was most favorable to agriculture. Out of the rich soil, tobacco and hemp grew plentifully.

The slaves lived in cabins at the back of the farm where the overseer, Grove Cook, had his house, too. Grove Cook was completely in charge of the plantation. He had no wife or family, so a slave woman kept house for him. She was responsible for giving out the supplies of food for the field hands. Another woman stayed all day in the slave quarters to cook for the field hands.

These field hands were called to their hard labor every morning at four o'clock, when the overseer rang a loud bell that hung from a post near his house. The slaves were only allowed half an hour to eat breakfast and get out to the fields. At four thirty, the overseer blew a horn as a signal to start working. If a slave got to the field after the horn blew, he received ten lashes from a whip the overseer always carried with him. It was a mean whip. The handle was about three feet long, with the heavy butt end full of lead. The lash itself was about six or seven feet of cowhide with a braid of wire at the tip. That whip was put to use often and freely. The overseer would lash a slave for even the smallest offense.

During the years Mr. Cook was overseer, I was a house servant. That was better than being a field hand. I ate better food, wore better clothes—and did not have to get up when the bell rang at four; I could stay in bed until four thirty. Lying in bed that extra half-hour, I often heard the crack of the whip and the screams of a slave in the field.

My mother was a field hand. One morning she was late getting out. She arrived at the field about ten or fifteen minutes after the others were already in their places. As soon as she got to her place, the overseer started to whip her. She cried for mercy.

"Oh! pray—Oh! pray—Oh! pray—"

Those are the words slaves use when they beg for mercy. I heard her voice. I recognized it and leaped out of my bed and ran to the door. The field was far from the house, but I could hear every crack of the whip and every cry and moan of my poor mother. I stayed there at the door. I did not dare to go out and try to help her. Cold chills ran through me and the tears streamed down my face. I sobbed out loud as I counted the lash strokes . . . three, four, five, six . . . After ten, the sound of the whip stopped. I turned and went back to my bed, weeping in the dark. It was not daylight yet.

Two

My master was a clever politician and people in the
town were ready to vote him into public office so that he
could do them favors. A few years after he settled in
Missouri, he was elected to a seat in the state legislature.
This meant that when the legislature was in session, my
master was away from the farm for months at a time.
While he was away, he left Mr. Cook in complete charge.
The overseer was cruel enough when the master was
home but much worse when he was away.

Among the field hands on the farm was a man named

Randall. He was at least six feet tall and very well built; everyone knew how strong and powerful he was. Randall was considered the most valuable worker of all the field slaves. No matter how good or useful they are, though, very few slaves manage to avoid flogging. But Randall had been on the farm ever since I could remember and I had never heard of his being whipped. That was not because of any kindness on the part of the master or the overseer but because of Randall himself. I often heard him say that he would die before any white man whipped him.

From the time Cook first came to the farm, he had boasted that he could and would whip any nigger who worked for him. My master warned him many times not to try to whip Randall but Cook was determined to try. As soon as the master put him in charge of the farm, he decided the time had come to put his threat into action. Dr. Young had only been away a few days when Cook began to find fault with everything Randall did and to threaten him with the whip if he did not do better. One day he set Randall to a bigger job than he could possibly do. At sundown Randall had only half-finished the work.

"I'll remember that tomorrow morning," said Cook.

The next morning after breakfast, Cook called Randall and told him he was going to be whipped.

"Why do you want to whip me?" Randall asked.

"Because you did not finish your work yesterday," Cook answered.

"I would have, but the job was too big," said Randall.

"That makes no difference," Cook answered. "I'm going to whip you anyway."

Randall stood silent for a moment. Then he said:

"Mr. Cook, I have always tried to please you since you have been on the plantation. I find you are determined not to be satisfied with my work no matter how well I do. No man has laid hands on me to whip me for the last ten years and long ago I decided not to be whipped by any man alive."

The overseer understood that Randall would resist the flogging so he called three field hands to seize Randall and tie him up. As soon as Cook gave the order, Randall turned to the field hands:

"Boys, you all know me. You know that I can handle any three of you, and I will kill any man who lays a hand on me. This white man cannot whip me himself. That is why he called on you to help him."

The field hands stood still. They knew Randall—they also knew how powerfully strong he was and were afraid to tangle with him. Nothing the overseer said or did could get those men to come near Randall. Finally he ordered them all into the fields.

For a week, things were quiet. Then one morning after the hands were already at work, Cook came into the fields with three husky white friends. All four were carrying clubs. They went up to the row where Randall was working. Cook told him to stop what he was doing and go with them to the barn. When Randall refused, the four white men attacked him. Randall fought back and was knocking them down, one after another, when one of the men drew a pistol and fired at him. Randall fell to the ground. The men rushed at him with their clubs and beat him over the head and on his face until finally they managed to tie him up. Then they hauled him off to the barn and strapped him to a beam. Cook gave him more than a hundred lashes with a heavy cowhide whip, then had him washed down with salt water and left him tied there all day and night. The next morning, Randall was untied and taken to a blacksmith's shop where a ball and chain were fastened to his leg. He was sent back to the field and forced to do the same amount of work as the other hands. When the master came back home, he was very pleased to find out that while he was away, Randall had finally broken down.

When I was almost fifteen years old, my master moved again, this time to the city of St. Louis. My young master, William, was by now a stout boy of five. He had seldom been disciplined by the doctor or his wife or Aunt Dolly, his nurse, who had been forbidden to restrain him. As a result, he had become impudent, petulant, peevish, and cruel. At the supper table, he often wanted to make an entire meal out of candy, the sugar bowl or the cake. When the mistress refused him his pleasure, he went into a fit of anger and threw anything within his reach at me: spoons, knives, forks and dishes

14

would be thrown at my head accompanied by language that would astonish anyone who did not know the way slavery affected the children of slave owners. This influence was noted by Thomas Jefferson in a letter he wrote to a friend in Paris in 1788. Jefferson wrote:

The parent storms, the child looks on, catches the lineaments of wrath, puts on the same airs in the circle of smaller slaves, gives loose to his worst passions; and, thus nursed, educated and daily exercised in tyranny, cannot but be stamped by it with odious peculiarities.

St. Louis is one of the most important cities in the country. It is located close to the mouth of the Missouri River. Across the river is the Free State of Illinois, where fugitive slaves make their first dash for freedom. Sometimes kindly white and black men give them food and shelter and hiding places and help them on their way further north, but too often both white and black slave chasers hunt down the runaways. According to fugitive slave laws, slaves are still the property of their masters even in Free States. The slave chasers get good rewards for their cruel work of capturing escaped slaves and returning them to St. Louis.

At St. Louis, the Missouri River connects with the upper Mississippi River, and steamboats with their paddle wheels go back and forth between St. Louis and New Orleans. The state of Missouri does a large commerce in slave breeding to supply hands for the big new cotton plantations spreading all over the Deep South, and New Orleans is the most important of all the slave-trading markets because it is the port where cargo ships unload their cargoes of slaves. Slaves costing one thousand dollars in St. Louis sell for fifteen hundred dollars on the New Orleans market. Slaves who are sold in New Orleans are shipped to plantations all through the lower South.

St. Louis on the Missouri River is also the best water route to the West, and settlers and adventurers in great numbers board steamers to travel westward. In addition to such settlers, the steamboats carry luxury goods for merchants to sell and raw materials for new factories.

St. Louis is the frontier city for overland travel, too. The covered wagons going westward are common sights in the city. About forty-five hundred people lived there when I was young. But with thousands of steamboats plying their commerce through the years, it must now have as many as ten or twenty thousand people.

In addition to his house in St. Louis, my master bought a farm about four miles out of the city and hired as overseer a Yankee from New England named Friend Haskell. I was glad I did not have to work for Haskell. Yankees are well known to be the cruelest overseers.

When my master was settled in St. Louis, he found that he had more slaves than he needed to keep the house running or help him in his medical practice. So he rented some of us to other masters. The practice of renting slaves was called "hiring out." I was hired out to a Major Freeland, who owned a hotel. Major Freeland, who came from Virginia, was a horse racer, cock fighter, gambler and drunkard. There were ten or twelve servants in the house and when he was present, it was cut and slash, knock down and drag out. When he was angry, he would pick up a chair and throw it at one of the slaves. In his more rational moments, when he wanted to punish a slave, he would tie him up in the smokehouse where they cured meat, whip him, order a fire of tobacco stems to be lit near him and then leave him to breathe in the smoke until he almost suffocated.

I complained to Dr. Young about the treatment I got from Major Freeland but it did not make any difference. My master did not care how many chairs were thrown at me or how often I was whipped so long as Major Freeland paid him for my work. He had hired me out the way he would hire out a horse he owned. He knew Major Freeland wanted to get his money's worth.

After living at Major Freeland's hotel for five or six months, I ran away. I went into the woods beyond the city and hid there all day. When night came, I made my way the four miles to Dr. Young's farm. Once there, though, I was afraid to be seen. I knew that if Mr. Haskell, the overseer, found me, he would take me back to Major Freeland. So I stayed in the woods. I stayed there, hiding, for several days. But one day I heard the barking and howling of dogs. They were coming nearer and I

realized they were the bloodhounds of Major Benjamin
O'Fallon. He kept five or six dogs to hunt runaway slaves
and my master had sent for them to find me.

As soon as I was sure the dogs were O'Fallon's blood-
hounds, I knew there was no chance to escape. I climbed
to the top of a tree. In minutes, the dogs were at the foot
of the tree. They stayed there, yelping and leaping up,
trying to reach me, for almost an hour until the hunters
came up. The two hunters ordered me to come down
from the tree. When I did, they tied me up and took me
to the St. Louis jail.

Major Freeland soon showed up at the jail, arranged
for my release, and ordered me to follow him, which I
did. When we got back to the hotel, I was tied to the
whipping post in the smokehouse and flogged. The lash
cut over my shoulders, under my arms, on my head and
ears. After the Major had flogged me to his satisfaction,
he told his son, Robert, to see that I was well smoked.
Robert built the fire of tobacco stems. While I was cough-
ing and sneezing, Robert told me that this was what his
father had learned to do to slaves in Virginia. He called
it "Virginia Play." After I had what they thought was a
decent smoking, I was untied and sent back to work.

Robert Freeland was a chip off the old block. Although he was quite young, he often staggered home as
drunk as his father. I believe he is now the popular captain of a steamboat on the Mississippi.

Shortly after my "smoking," Major Freeland's hotel

18

failed and I was sent back to Dr. Young, who promptly hired me out to serve Captain William B. Culver aboard the steamship *Missouri*. Like all river boats, the *Missouri* was a wide, shallow vessel with three decks, the deck for freight being nearest the water, then the passenger deck, and above that, the light hurricane deck and a pilot-house. The top of the boat had the smokestacks. I stayed on her all through the sailing season, and it was as pleasant a time as I had ever known.

Life on the Mississippi River is an exciting one. I had not been on the boat a few weeks before one of those races for which the southern steamboats are so famous took place. At eight o'clock one evening, we saw the lights of another steamboat in the distance. It apparently was coming up very fast. This was the signal for general excitement on board our boat, and everything indicated that a race was at hand. Soon the boats were side by side, each trying to get ahead of the other. The night was clear, the moon was shining brightly, and the boats were so close to each other that the passengers were within speaking distance.

On the *Missouri*, the firemen were using oil, lard, butter, and even bacon to raise the steam to its hottest pitch. The blaze mingled with the black smoke that came from the smokestacks of the other boat, which showed that she, too, was burning something that blazed more than wood. The firemen of both boats, who were slaves, were singing songs such as can be heard only on board a southern

steamboat. Now the boats came closer and closer to each
other until they were locked so that men could go from
one to the other. The wildest fervor existed among the
men who worked on the boat, and the passengers shared
the excitement.

At this moment, the engineer of our boat fastened
down the safety valve so that no steam could escape.
This made the engine hotter so it would go faster but it
was indeed a dangerous thing to do. A few people who
saw what he had done were afraid that there would be
an explosion and left that part of the boat for safer
quarters.

The *Missouri* stopped to take on passengers but still
no steam was allowed to escape. When the boat was
started again, cold water was forced into the boilers and,
as might have been expected, one boiler exploded with
terrific force. The explosion blew up part of the lower
deck and tore much of the machinery to pieces. A dense
fog of steam filled every part of the vessel and shrieks,
groans and cries were heard everywhere. Men were
running back and forth looking for their wives, and
women were flying around in wild confusion looking for
their husbands. Dismay appeared on every face.

The lounges and cabins soon resembled hospitals
more than anything else, but in a very short time, the
boat drifted to shore and the killed and wounded, numbering nineteen, were taken off. The other steamer came
alongside to help us and soon the *Missouri*, towed by the

boat she had raced, was once again on her journey.

It was half past twelve and the passengers, instead of going to their berths, gathered at the gambling tables. To see five or six tables in the saloon of a steamer with half a dozen men playing cards at each, and money, pistols and bowie knives spread around in splendid confusion is an ordinary thing on the Mississippi River. The practice of gambling on the river has long been annoying to more moral people who travel by steamboat. Thousands of dollars in cash and merchandise often change owners during a trip from St. Louis, or Louisville, to New Orleans on a Mississippi steamer. Many men are completely wiped out, and duels are often fought.

"Go call my boy, steward," said Mr. Jones on this particular occasion as he took his cards one by one from the table.

In a few minutes a fine-looking bright-eyed mulatto boy, about sixteen years old, was standing by his master's side at the table.

"I am broke, all but my boy, Joe," said Jones as he ran his fingers through his cards, "but he is worth a thousand dollars and I will bet the half of him."

"I will call you," said Thompson as he laid five hundred dollars at the feet of the boy who was now standing on the table. At the same time he threw his cards down.

"You have beaten me," said Jones. The other gentlemen laughed as poor Joe stepped down from the table.

"Well, I suppose I owe you half the nigger," said Thompson as he took hold of Joe and started to examine his arms and legs.

"Yes," said Jones, "he is half yours. Let me have five hundred dollars and I will give you a bill of sale for him."

"Go back to your bed," said Thompson to his chattel, "and remember that you now belong to me."

The poor slave wiped the tears from his eyes as he turned obediently to leave.

"My father gave me that boy," said Jones as he took the money. "I hope, Mr. Thompson, that you will allow me to redeem him."

"Most certainly, sir," said Thompson, "whenever you hand over the cool thousand, the Negro is yours."

Next morning, as the passengers were coming into the lounge and on deck and the slaves were running around waiting on or looking for their masters, poor Joe was seen entering his new master's stateroom, boots in hand.

Such is the uncertainty of a slave's life. He goes to bed at night the pampered servant of the young master who played with him as a child and would not let his slave be abused for anything, and gets up in the morning the property of a man he has never seen before.

Three

When winter brought an end to the sailing season, I was
hired out to another hotelkeeper, Mr. John Colburn. He
was from one of the Free States, but I do not think any
man ever hated Negroes more than he did.

The hotel, the Missouri Hotel, was one of the largest
in the city and hired about twenty or thirty servants,
mostly slaves. Mr. Colburn was cruel to them all. He
also ill-treated his wife, who was an excellent woman. I
never heard her speak a harsh word to a servant; I never
heard her husband speak a kind word.

Among the slaves hired out to the hotel was a man named Aaron who belonged to Mr. John Darby, a lawyer. Aaron was the knife-washer. One day, one of the knives on the table was not as clean as it might have been. For this offense, Mr. Colburn tied Aaron to a beam in the woodshed and gave him fifty lashes on his bare back with a cowhide whip. Then he made me pour rum over Aaron, which seemed to give him more pain than the whipping.

When Aaron was untied, he went home to his master, Mr. Darby, and told him about the harsh treatment. Mr. Darby would not even listen to anything Aaron said but sent him straight back. When Colburn heard that Aaron had complained to Mr. Darby, the slave was tied up again and given a whipping worse than the first one. The poor fellow's back was literally cut to pieces and he could not work for almost two weeks.

One evening, Mr. Colburn whipped a servant girl named Patsey so brutally that several of the hotel boarders came out to the woodshed and begged him to stop. The reason for the whipping was simply this: Patsey was engaged to marry John, a man belonging to Major William Christy who lived four or five miles north of the city. Mr. Colburn had forbidden her to see John—people said it was because Colburn liked her himself.

Patsey had gone to a prayer meeting that evening and John walked her home. Colburn had threatened to flog

John if he came inside the gate and John, who knew his rival's temper, had kept a safe distance away. When Patsey came in, Colburn had taken all his fury out on the poor girl.

If all the slave drivers in the country had been gathered into one group, I do not think any of them could have been crueler than John Colburn—and he a northerner.

While I was living at Mr. Colburn's hotel, an event took place that caused me much sorrow. My master sold my mother and all of her children except me. He sold them in the city of St. Louis.

After a few months, I was taken away from Mr. Colburn and sent to serve Elijah J. Lovejoy, a publisher and the editor of the *St. Louis Times*. I worked mostly in the printing office, running errands for the pressmen and sometimes operating the presses myself. Mr. Lovejoy was a very good man. In 1837, three years after my escape to freedom, he became the editor of an abolitionist newspaper and was foully murdered for his views by a mob of slaveholders.

The little learning I acquired in slavery I owe entirely to Mr. Lovejoy. He introduced me to education. But Mr. Lovejoy did not educate me about slavery. I learned myself. Most people think that slavery is milder in Missouri than in the cotton- sugar- and rice-growing states. But they are wrong. Missouri has slave-breeding farms and no slaveholding section of this country contains crueler people than the citizens of St. Louis. It was in St. Louis that an officer of the United States Army, a Colonel Harney, whipped a slave woman to death. In St. Louis, a gang of slave owners hauled a free Negro, a Pittsburgh man named Francis McIntosh, from the steamboat *Flora* and burned him at the stake. I lived in this city for eight years and with my own eyes saw so many acts of violence I could not begin to list them all on these pages. But I will give a few more examples.

A neighbor of my master, a Captain Brunt, owned a slave named John, who was his body servant and drove his carriage. One day, John was driving Captain Brunt through town. It had just stopped raining and John was keeping the horses at a quick pace. When the carriage passed along the streets, it happened to splatter some mud upon a gentleman named Robert Moore. Moore swore revenge. Three or four months later, he bought John for the express purpose, as he explained, "to tame the damned nigger." Immediately after the sale, he took John to a blacksmith and had a ball and chain fastened to his leg. Then he set John to driving a team of oxen. He kept the slave at active labor until the leg iron wore so deeply into the flesh that festering began. John told me that in addition to the irons, his master whipped him regularly three times a week for the first two months. All this was to "tame him" for splashing some mud. John was as noble-looking a man as any to be seen in St. Louis before he fell into the hands of Moore. After he had been "tamed" for three months, he looked more degraded and broken in spirit than a slave from the worst southern plantation. The last time I saw him, he had lost nearly all the use of his legs.

I, too, had an experience with revenge. Mr. Lovejoy occasionally sent me on errands to the office of another newspaper, the *Missouri Republican*. One winter afternoon he sent me there to bring back a font of type—that is, the heavy metal letters that are used for printing. On my way back, I was attacked by several white boys, all bigger than I was and all the sons of slaveholders. They began by throwing hard snowballs at me. With the box of heavy type in my hands, I could not run away from them. I had no choice but to lay the box down and fight back. But they soon circled around me, throwing stones and hitting me with sticks. As they came closer, I knew they would catch me and beat me, so I took to my heels. After I escaped, they captured the box of type. I did not know what to do to get it back. But I knew Mr. Lovejoy was a humane man, so I went to him at his office and explained what had happened. He had me wait while he and one of the apprentice printers went out to find the boys. They soon came back with the box of type, but Mr. Lovejoy told me that Samuel McKinney had promised to whip me because, during the brief battle, I had hurt his son. Almost as soon as the words were out of Mr. Lovejoy's mouth, one of the printers saw McKinney striding toward the office. I was warned just in time to escape through the back door.

When McKinney arrived and realized I had got away, he stormed out of the office in a great rage, announcing that he would whip me to death when he found me. A few days later, as I was walking down Main Street, he did find me. He grabbed me by the collar and hit me on the head five or six times with a heavy cane he carried. Blood gushed from my nose and ears. Blood flooded my clothes. When he finally beat me to his satisfaction, he let me go. I managed to stagger back to the office, but I was so weak from loss of blood that Mr. Lovejoy sent me home to my master to get well. It was five weeks before I was able to walk again. During that time, Mr. Lovejoy needed someone to do my work. He hired another boy and I lost the best job—and the best master—I ever had.

After I got well, Dr. Young hired me out to Captain Otis Reynolds as a waiter on board the steamboat *Enterprise,* which was owned by Messrs. John and Edward Walsh, St. Louis men whose business was to buy and sell merchandise on commission. The boat ran on the upper Mississippi. My job was to wait on gentlemen and since the captain was a good man, it was pleasant for me. But sailing from port to port, seeing new people every day and knowing that they could go wherever they pleased, saddened me. Several times I thought about leaving the boat when it tied up at some port and trying to escape to Canada, where I had heard a slave might live free and protected.

But whenever I was tempted to run off, I would remember that my mother was a slave in St. Louis. I could not bear the idea of freedom for myself and not for her. When I thought about how she had suffered so much for my sake, I would swear to myself that I would never leave the land of slavery without her. It was the least I owed her. Besides, in addition to my mother, I had three brothers and a sister who were slaves in St. Louis. Two of my brothers had died.

My mother, my brothers Joseph and Millford, and my sister Elizabeth all belonged to Mr. Isaac Mansfield, who came from one of the Free States—Massachusetts, I think. He was a tinsmith with a large manufacturing establishment. Of all my relatives, I felt closest to my mother and then to my sister. One evening when I was visiting them, I made some comment about a trip to Canada. Elizabeth came over to me and took my hand. There were tears in her eyes.

"Brother, you are not going to leave your mother and your dear sister here without a friend," she said.

I looked into her face. Seeing tears now streaming down her cheeks, I burst into tears myself.

"No, I will never desert you and mother," I exclaimed.

She was still for a moment. Then she said, "Brother, you have often declared you would not end your days in slavery. I see no possible way you can escape with us." She held my hand tighter. "Now, brother, you are on a steamboat where there is some chance for you to escape.

I beg you not to let us hold you back. Even if we cannot be free, we do not want to keep you from freedom."

I was so upset I made her stop talking about it. Fervently, I told them that even if they wanted me to break away and leave them behind, I would not do so. I pledged I would not. I said good night to them and went back to the boat. It was late at night, but when I lay down on my bunk, I could not sleep.

Four

A few weeks later, as we were going downriver, the boat stopped at Hannibal, Missouri, and took on board a gang of slaves bound for the New Orleans slave market. There were fifty or sixty men and women ranging in age from about eighteen to forty. A gang of slaves on a southern steamboat headed for cotton or sugar states is such a common occurrence that usually no one, not even the passengers, seems to notice, even though the slaves' chains clank noisily at every step. But in this group, there was a slave who attracted everybody's attention.

She was a beautiful girl, about twenty years old, perfectly white with straight light hair and blue eyes. It was not her fairness that created the sensation, however. It was her almost unparalleled beauty. She had only been on the boat a little while before all the passengers, including the ladies, noticed and began to talk about the beautiful slave girl.

The man who claimed this article of human merchandise was Mr. Walker, a well-known slave trader who lived in St. Louis. The passengers and crew were greatly curious to learn about the girl, but Mr. Walker kept close to her. It would have been considered impudent for a passenger to speak to her and the crew was forbidden to talk to the slaves, so when we reached St. Louis and the slave gang was loaded onto the boat going to New Orleans, the history of the girl was still a mystery.

During the summer season, when I was on the boat, we often took on board gangs of slaves on their way to the cotton, sugar and rice plantations in the South. It is a terrible fate for slaves. There is very little humanity for them on southern plantations. They each have only one set of clothes which they often wear until it is worn off, for they are allowed no time for washing clothes. For food, they fare badly. They are given no more meal or meat than will keep them able to work. They never get sugar or butter or cheese or milk. The worst thing is that they are worked like herds of human cattle. The overseer is only concerned with getting them to produce

the greatest possible crop. Picking cotton, slaves are as-
signed an amount to bring in at the end of the day. You
see the field slaves, with their baskets of cotton, slowly
wending their way up to the cotton house, where each
one's basket is weighed. They have no means of knowing, in the course of the day, how much they pick, so they
are in suspense until their basket is weighed.

"So many pounds short," cries the overseer, and he
takes up his whip and the lash is applied.

Toward the end of the summer, Captain Reynolds left
the boat and I was sent home. Instead of being hired out
again, I was now sent to Dr. Young's farm to work as a
field hand under Mr. Haskell, the overseer. I had not
been in the fields for many months. I was not used to
working in the burning sun and it was especially hard
because I was forced to keep pace with the best of the
field hands.

There was a great difference between work in the
cabin of a steamboat and work in a cornfield.

In early winter, my master left St. Louis and moved
his family to the farm, and I was called from the fields
to work in the house as a waiter. My master's wife was
very ill-tempered and hard to please, but I much preferred working for her than for the overseer. Two guests
joined the family on the farm that year. One, Miss
Martha Tulley, was a niece of theirs from Kentucky.
The other was Mr. Sloane, a young Presbyterian minister
who had been in the South only a short time. His whole

aim in life seemed to be to please slaveholders, especially my master and mistress. I think he succeeded very well. When they wanted to sing, he sang. When they wanted to listen to a story, he told a story. When they wanted some praying, he prayed. But he did not teach my master religion. Instead, my master taught religion to him.

While I had been away working for Captain Reynolds on the steamboat, my master had "got religion." In addition to teaching the minister, he made new laws for the farm. Before the new laws, Sundays had been easy days, when we could hunt or go fishing or just sit around, weaving splint brooms and baskets and enjoying sociability. Now all that was stopped. Every Sunday we had to attend meeting. My master had become so religious that he persuaded other slave owners to join him in hiring a preacher to preach to the slaves.

A preacher I remember was a low, squatty man about forty years old, who had been born in upstate New York and, having once been a sailor, talked and acted with all the roughness of seafaring men.

About eleven o'clock every Sunday morning, he would drive his one-horse wagon and charge up to the trees near the slave quarters where the slaves had been gathered since sunup waiting for him. He was supposed to come early. Almost before the horse stopped moving, the preacher jumped out of the wagon and took his place at the foot of one of the trees, where a sort of rough

34

board table was set up. Pulling his books from his pocket, he pitched right in. There was some singing and there was some praying but there was a lot of preaching.

The minister would preach for a while about every soul's duty to the great Master in Heaven. Then he would preach about the duties of slaves to their masters and mistresses here on earth.

"Take care that you do not fret or murmur, grumble or repine at your condition; for this will not only make your life uneasy, but it will greatly offend Almighty God. Consider that it is not yourself, not the people that you belong to, it is not the men who have brought you to it but it is the will of God who hath made you servants, because, no doubt, he knew that condition would be best for you in this world and help you the better towards heaven. You ought always to carry in your minds one general rule—to do all service for your masters and mistresses as if you did them for God himself.

"And surely you should serve your masters faithfully because of their goodness to you. See to what trouble they have been on your account. Your fathers were poor, ignorant and barbarous creatures in Africa and the whites fitted out ships at great trouble and expense and brought you from that benighted land to Christian America, where you can sit under your own vine and fig tree and no one molest or make you afraid."

The preacher slammed his fist down on the board table like a sledge-hammer. He swung his arms and shouted till his face turned red. But for all his effort, he could not keep the slaves interested. Four or five of them would just go to sleep, leaning against the trees. Five or six others nodded, trying to stay awake. Some, gazing directly at the preacher, secretly cracked hazelnuts and popped them into their mouths.

My master held family prayer meetings night and morning. At night the servants were called in to attend, but in the mornings, when they had to be at work, it was just family worship. Dr. and Mrs. Young were great lovers of mint julep, and every morning a big pitcher was made with plenty of whiskey. The whole family drank freely, even little Master William. After many cups of julep they would have worship, and then go to breakfast. As I was their waiter, I was always there. I must say that I liked mint julep as much as they did. During prayer meeting, I was careful to sit close to the table with the pitcher on it so I could help myself steadily while they were busy at their devotions. By the time the praying was over, I was as happy as any of them.

One morning, though, there was a sad accident. I was helping myself to julep and at the same time keeping an eye on my old mistress when I accidentally dropped the pitcher. It hit the floor and broke into pieces, spilling mint julep everywhere. It was a bad business. As soon as the meeting was over, I was taken out and severely punished.

Among my duties to the family was to drive them to church in the city, four miles away. I always dreaded Sundays because while they were at church, I had to stand on the street with the horses in the broiling sun or in the pouring rain, if it happened to be raining.

One Sunday we drove past the house of Mr. D. D. Page, a rich man who owned a large bakery. My driver's seat was very high on the carriage and I could see Mr. Page holding a long whip and chasing a slave around the yard. He lashed out at the poor fellow, cutting his flesh at every jump. The slave dashed furiously out of the yard with Mr. Page following after him. They came running past us. When the slave realized he was going to be overtaken, he stopped suddenly and Mr. Page fell over him onto the stone pavement. The tumble broke one of his legs. That break never mended right and Mr. Page limped for the rest of his life. I did not feel sorry for him. He was a deacon in the Baptist church, in good and regular standing, but a few weeks earlier he had tied up a woman slave, Delphia, and whipped her nearly to death. Poor Delphia! I knew her very well and went to visit her when she was on her sickbed recovering from that whipping. I will never forget the way she looked. And Delphia was a member of the same Baptist church as her master.

Soon after this, I was hired out to Mr. Walker, the same man I had seen shipping a gang of slaves to New Orleans when I was on the *Enterprise*. Walker had noticed me working as a steward and had decided I would be a good man to look after slaves. He tried to buy me for the job but when my master would not sell me, he hired me instead. The contract was for a year. Later I heard that Mr. Walker had offered a high price when he tried to buy me. I suppose Dr. Young did not sell me because I was his relative.

Five

When I learned that I had been hired out to a Negro speculator—or a soul driver, as slaves called them—I realized I had lost my chance to escape to freedom, at least for the time being. When I started to work for Mr. Walker, he had a gang of slaves all ready to start for New Orleans, and in a few days we were on our way. I cannot find words to express how I felt as we set off. Although my master had told me he did not sell me and Mr. Walker had told me he did not buy me, I did not believe either of them. Not until I had been in New Orleans and was on the boat coming back was I convinced I had not been sold.

On the boat, the slaves were kept in a large room on the lower deck, men and women casually jammed together. They were chained, two by two, and watched carefully to make sure they did not get loose. There have been cases of slaves who have slipped out of their chains and escaped at landing places while boats were taking on wood for their furnaces. Despite all our care, we lost one woman who had been sold away from her husband and child. She did not want to live without them and, in the agony of her soul, jumped overboard and drowned. She was one of the few slaves who were not chained.

It was almost impossible to keep that part of the boat clean.

When we landed in Natchez, Tennessee, we took all the slaves to the slave pen and, by the time we left at the end of a week, had sold several of them. Mr. Walker fed his slaves well. In St. Louis he had shipped on board a few hundred pounds of bacon and cornmeal. As far as I could tell, his slaves had better food than most slaves in Natchez.

Two days after leaving Natchez, we arrived in New Orleans, the end of our journey. Here the slaves were put into the Negro pen where anybody interested in buying could come and examine them. The slave pen is a small yard, fifteen to twenty feet wide, surrounded by buildings. It has only one outside entrance, a large gate with strong iron bars. Slaves are kept in the buildings at night and turned out into the yard during the day. After the best of the slaves were sold privately at the pen, we took the rest to the Exchange Coffee House Auction Rooms, where they were sold at public auction.

The less valuable slaves were placed first on the auction block, one after another, and sold to the highest bidder. Husbands and wives were separated with a degree of indifference unknown in any area of life except slavery. Brothers and sisters were torn from each other. Mothers saw their children leave them for the rest of their lives.

Among our slaves was a young girl. The auctioneer reserved her for the last.

"She is last because she is valuable," cried the auctioneer. "How much, gentlemen? Fit for a fancy girl for anyone. She enjoys good health. Has a sweet temper. How much do you say?"

"Five hundred," one man called out.

"Only five hundred for such a girl as this? Gentlemen, she's worth a good deal more than that. Here, gentlemen, I hold in my hand a paper certifying that she has a good moral character."

"Seven hundred."

"This paper also states that she is very intelligent."

"Eight hundred."

"She is a devoted Christian and perfectly trust-worthy."

"Nine hundred."

"Nine fifty."

"Ten."

"Eleven."

The sale came to a standstill. The auctioneer stopped, looked around and told a rough story about selling slaves. It was a strange scene. The crowd was laughing and swearing, smoking and spitting and talking in a steady hum of noise while the slave girl stood with tears in her eyes glancing at the men who were bidding for her.

"Twelve."

"Thirteen."

"Thirteen fifty."

"Thirteen fifty," cried the auctioneer and the sale was made. With the last of the slaves sold, we left New Orleans and went back to St. Louis.

As soon as we arrived in St. Louis, I went to Dr. Young and told him I did not want to stay with Mr. Walker any more. It made me sick at heart to see my fellow human beings bought and sold. But the doctor had hired me out for the year and I had to go back.

Mr. Walker immediately began buying up a gang of slaves. One man he bought belonged to Colonel John O'Fallon who lived in the suburbs of St. Louis. The man had a wife and three children. As soon as the sale was made, Mr. Walker put him in jail for safekeeping until we were ready to leave for New Orleans. His wife came to visit him there several times, but often the jailer refused to let her see him.

In eight or nine weeks, Mr. Walker had his full cargo of human flesh. Among them were a number of older men and women, some already gray-headed. On the boat, I had to get these old slaves ready for market before we reached our first stop. I was ordered to shave off the old men's whiskers and to pluck out the gray hairs, if there were not too many of them. Otherwise, I was to dye the gray hair with a bottle of blacking and a brush Walker gave me. This was a new business for me. It took place in a room where the passengers could not see us. In addition, the slaves were taught to lie about their age.

"How old are you?" Mr. Walker asked a man who looked no less than forty.

"If I live to see next corn-planting time I will be either forty-five or fifty-five, I don't know which."

"That may be. But now you are only thirty years old."

"I know I am more than that," said the man.

"When you get in the market and anybody asks you how old you are and you tell them forty-five, I will tie you up and whip you like smoke. But if you tell them you are only thirty, then I won't."

"Well, then, I guess I will only be thirty when they ask me."

After the hair-dyeing process, they appeared ten or fifteen years younger. Few white people can come anywhere near guessing the age of a Negro just by looking, so slave traders usually get by with this trick. Some of the people who bought from Mr. Walker were badly cheated about the ages of their new slaves.

We landed at Rodney, where we drove the slaves to the pen in the back part of the village and in four or five days sold a few. Then we took the rest back to the boat and went on to Natchez. We landed there at night and put the gang in the warehouse until morning when we herded them to the pen. As soon as slaves appeared in these pens, swarms of planters showed up. They knew when Mr. Walker would arrive because he always advertised ahead of time when he would be in Rodney, Natchez and New Orleans, his three best markets.

At Natchez this second time, I saw a slave who had been very cruelly whipped. The slave, Lewis, was originally from St. Louis and I had known him for several years. He belonged to a merchant named Broadwell, the owner of a store on the wharf. Mr. Walker sent me to the wharf to watch for the boat that would take us to New Orleans and to let him know when it arrived. While I was waiting, I went into Mr. Broadwell's store to visit Lewis. I asked a slave I saw there where Lewis was.

"They have him hanging between heaven and earth," the slave said.

"What do you mean?" I asked.

"Go into the warehouse and see," he answered.

I went in and found Lewis. He was tied by his wrists to a beam, with his toes just touching the floor. There was nobody else in the warehouse, so I asked him what happened. He told me that Mr. Broadwell had sold his wife to a planter six miles from Natchez. Lewis had tried to visit her at night and, since he planned to get back before daylight, had not gotten his master's permission. The patrol that watches for runaway slaves had caught him before he reached his wife and put him in jail. They got in touch with his master who had to pay for his catching and keeping, and that is what he was tied up for.

Just as Lewis finished his story, Mr. Broadwell came in and asked what I was doing there. While I tried to think of what to say, he hit me on the head with the butt of his whip. It landed just above my right eye and cut so deep that I still have the scar. Lewis had had fifty lashes before I saw him. He told me later that Mr. Broadwell gave him fifty lashes more after I left.

The next day we went on to New Orleans and put the slave gang into the same Negro pen we had used before.

Before the slaves were displayed for sale, they were dressed and driven out into the yard. Some were made to dance, some to jump around, some to play cards. The idea was to make them seem cheerful and happy. My job was to see that this was done before the buyers arrived and I have often forced slaves to dance when their cheeks were wet with tears. When buyers examined Walker's merchandise, they would tell the slaves to walk back and forth and would feel their hands and arms and bodies, turn them around, ask them what work they could do, make them open their mouths and show their teeth just the way a man examines a horse he is planning to trade or buy. Sometimes a man or woman is taken into one of the buildings, stripped and inspected more carefully. Scars upon a slave's back are considered proof of a rebellious or unruly spirit and hurt his sale.

Slaves were in good demand on that trip. Soon we sold them all and set off for St. Louis again.

Six

When we got back, Mr. Walker bought a farm for himself five or six miles outside the city. He had no family but made one of his female slaves keep house for him. Poor Cynthia. I knew her well. She was a quadroon, one of the most beautiful women I ever saw, and virtuous and well-mannered. Mr. Walker bought her for the New Orleans market and took her south on one of the trips I made with him. I will never forget that trip. The first night aboard, Mr. Walker told me to put her in a stateroom he had reserved for her separate from the other slaves. I had seen enough of the workings of slavery to know what that meant. I watched him go into the state-room and listened at the door. I heard him make his vile offer and heard her reject it. He told her that if she would be his mistress, he would take her back to St. Louis and set her up as his housekeeper. But if she refused, he would sell her as a field hand on the worst plantation along the river. Neither his threats nor his bribes worked, though, and he angrily left the cabin.

The next morning, Cynthia told me what happened and cried at her fate. I gave her all the comfort and encouragement I could, but I knew beforehand what the end had to be. Without going into more details, I will just say that Walker kept his side of the bargain for a while. He took her back to St. Louis and made her his mistress and the housekeeper of his farm. Before I left the South, he had two children by her. But that is not the full story. Since I have been away from there, I have heard reliably that Walker got married and to clear the way for his wife, sold poor Cynthia and their four children (they had two more after I had gone) into hopeless bondage!

Walker now started gathering a third gang of merchandise. We went by steamboat to Jefferson City, a town on the Missouri River, and by stagecoach into the middle of the state, buying up slaves as we passed different farms and villages. We had about twenty-two or twenty-three men and women when we got to the village of St. Charles on the banks of the river. There he bought a woman who had a child about four or five weeks old in her arms.

We hoped to find a boat at St. Charles to take us to St. Louis, but it turned out that no boat was expected for several days, so we went by land. Mr. Walker bought two horses. He rode one and I rode the other. We chained the slaves together and started marching in file, Mr. Walker at the head and I bringing up the rear. St. Louis was less than twenty miles away but we could not reach it in one day. The road was the worst I ever traveled on.

As we left St. Charles, the baby began to cry and kept crying for almost the whole day. Mr. Walker complained several times.

"Stop that child's damned noise or I will," he kept telling the mother.

She tried, but she could not hush the baby. That night we stayed with a family Mr. Walker knew, and in the morning, when we were setting out, the baby started to cry again. Mr. Walker stepped up to the mother and told her to give him the baby. She obeyed trembling. Walker took the child by one arm, the way you would take a cat by the leg, and walked into the house.

"Madam," he said to the lady there. "I make you a present of this little nigger. It keeps making so much noise I cannot bear it."

"Thank you, sir," said the lady.

When the mother saw that her child was going to be left behind, she ran to Mr. Walker and fell on her knees and clutched his legs and cried:

"Oh, my child! my child! Master, do let me have my child! Oh, do, do, do. I will stop its crying if you will only let me have it again."

When I saw this woman crying so pitifully for her child, I shuddered with a feeling close to horror. In the years since then, I have often heard still ringing in my ears the cries of that woman begging for her child.

Mr. Walker ordered her to join the other slaves. Women with children were not chained but those without children were. As soon as her baby was given away, this woman was chained into the gang.

We finally arrived at Mr. Walker's farm. While we were away, he had had a house built to put the slaves in. It was a kind of private jail. The slaves were locked in at night and worked on the farm during the day. They were kept there until the gang was complete. Then we started again for New Orleans. We had a large gang this time. Among them was a man named Joe. Mr. Walker was training Joe to take my place since my year was nearly over—and I was glad!

Our first stop was Vicksburg where we stayed one week and sold several slaves.

Mr. Walker was not a good master but he had not flogged a slave since I had been with him. He had threatened me a few times but only once did he come close to it. While the slaves were kept in the pen, Mr. Walker always stayed at the best hotel and kept good wines in his room to serve the men who came to see him about buying slaves. One day in Vicksburg, several gentlemen came calling and, as usual, Mr. Walker asked for the wine. I started passing the tray around. Accidentally, I had filled some of the glasses too full and when the men began to drink, they spilled wine on their clothes. Mr. Walker apologized to them for my carelessness, but from the way he looked at me, I knew that was not the end of the matter.

When the men left, he asked me just what I meant by being so careless and told me he would attend to me. The next morning he gave me a note to take to the jailer and a dollar bill to give to him. I had an idea that something was wrong, so I went down near the wharf and asked a sailor if he would be kind enough to read the note for me. He read it over and then glanced at me.

"What is in it?" I asked.

"They are going to give you hell," he said.

"Why?"

"This is a note to have you whipped and says that you have a dollar to pay for it."

It is a fact that in most slaveholding cities, a man who wants his slaves whipped can send them to the jail and have it done.

He handed back the note and off I went. I did not

know what to do but I decided I was not going to be whipped. I went up to the jail, took a look at it and walked off again. Mr. Walker knew the jailer and I was afraid that he would know if I did not show up at the jail and do something worse to me.

While I was thinking about my problem, a colored man just about my size walked by and I quickly thought of something. I walked up to him and asked him who he belonged to. He said he was a free man and had only been in the city a few days. I told him I had a note to go into the jail and get a trunk to take to one of the steamboats but that I was so busy I could not do it. I had a dollar to pay for it. He asked me for the job. I handed him my note and the dollar and he took off for the jail.

I watched to make sure he went in. As soon as the door closed behind him, I walked around the corner and waited to see how he looked when he came out. I had only been there a short time when a colored man walked by and said to another colored man:

"They're giving a nigger scissors in the jail."

"What for?" asked his friend.

"This nigger came into the jail and asked for the jailer. The jailer came out and he handed him a note and said he wanted to get a trunk. The jailer told him to come in and he would give him the trunk. So he took the nigger into the room and told him to give up the dollar. The nigger said a man had given him the dollar to pay for getting the trunk. But the jailer said that lie would not do. They made the nigger strip himself and then they tied him down and now are whipping him."

When I heard all that, I knew they were talking about my man. I crossed the street and hid opposite the jail so that nobody coming out would see me. Soon the young man appeared, looking for me. I left my hiding place behind a pile of bricks and stood before him. When he saw me, he was angry.

"You played a trick on me," he said.

"I did not know what was in the note," I said. "What did they do to you?"

He told me just about the same thing I had heard the colored man say.

"Yes," he said, "they whipped me and took my dollar and gave me this note."

He showed me the note the jailer had given him to take to his master.

"I will give you fifty cents for that note," I said. That was all the money I had.

He gave it to me and took his money. He had had twenty lashes on his bare back with the Negro whip.

With the note in my hand, I went back to Mr. Walker's hotel. In the lobby, I gave it to a stranger, a man I had not seen before, and asked him to read it to me. As I remember, it went something like this:

Dear Sir:—

By your direction, I have given your boy twenty lashes. He is a very saucy boy and tried to make out that he did not belong to you and I thrashed him well for lying to me.

I remain,
Your obedient servant.

Before I saw Mr. Walker, I wet my cheeks a little, as though I had been crying. He looked at me and asked what was the matter. I told him I never had had such a whipping in my life, and gave him the note. When he read it, he laughed.

"So you told him you did not belong to me."

"Yes, sir," I said. "I did not know there was any harm in that."

"Well, you behave yourself if you do not want to get whipped again," he said.

I think this story shows how slavery turns people into liars and cheats, then uses the lying and cheating to prove that slaves deserve their fate. Since my escape, I have often thought about the trick I played on that innocent fellow and been deeply sorry about it. I hope that some day I can make it up to him for the whipping he got in my place.

We arrived in New Orleans at night and stayed on board the boat until morning. From the deck that evening, I saw a slave killed.

It was some time between seven and eight o'clock when a colored man came running down the levee, chased by several white men and boys yelling:

"Stop that nigger! Stop that nigger!"

The slave kept gasping:

"I did not steal the meat, I did not steal the meat."

The poor man dove into the river for safety. The white men who were chasing him ran onto one of the boats tied up there to try to see him. They finally got a glimpse of him under the bow of one boat, the *Trenton*. With a long pole, they tried to prod him out of his hiding place. Whenever they struck at him, he dove under water. The water was very cold. It was clear that soon he had to come out or drown.

All the time they were trying to get him away from the bow of the boat—or to drown him—he cried out in a pitiful voice:

"I did not steal the meat. I did not steal the meat. My master lives up the river. I want to see my master. I did not steal the meat. Let me go home to my master."

The men kept hitting him over the head with the pole until finally he sank into the water and did not come up again.

At the end of the pole they were using was a hook that caught on his clothes and they hauled him up onto the deck. He lay still. Some of the men said he was playing possum and kicked him to make him get up. It was no use. He was dead.

When the men realized they had killed the slave, one by one they sneaked off the boat. A member of the boat's crew reported to the captain that a dead body was lying on the deck. The captain rushed up and collared the last of the men.

"You killed this nigger. Now take him off my boat."

The man dragged the body onto the shore and left it there.

All night I kept thinking about what I had seen. Early the next morning, I went on shore to see if the dead body was still there. It was in exactly the same position they had left it the night before. I waited to see what would happen to it. It stayed there, untouched, until about eight or nine o'clock when the cart that takes trash off the streets came along. The trashman simply threw the body in the cart and in a few minutes it was covered over with the dirt they were cleaning off the streets. During the whole time, I did not see more than six or seven people even notice the body. I guess it was not an unusual sight.

While we were in New Orleans, I met a young white man I had known very well in St. Louis. He had been sold into slavery several years before. This is how it happened. His father had been a drunk and very poor, with five or six children. When he died, the mother had to look after the family as well as she could. The oldest child, a boy named Burrill who was about thirteen years old, helped his mother by working in a store kept by a

Mr. Riley. He had been working for Mr. Riley two years when Riley went to New Orleans and took Burrill with him as his servant. Riley sold Burrill in New Orleans. When he came back to St. Louis, he told the boy's mother that Burrill had died of yellow fever in the South. Since nothing more was ever heard from the boy, nobody thought he was alive. I was astounded when Burrill told me all this. But even though I felt sorry for him, I could not help him in any way. We were both slaves. He was poor, uneducated and without friends. If he is still alive, I guess he is still a slave.

When we sold this cargo of human flesh, we went back to St. Louis and my time with Mr. Walker was over. I had served him one year. It was the longest year I ever lived.

Seven

When Mr. Walker dismissed me, I was glad to leave the
service of a man who tore husband from wife, child
from mother, sister from brother—but I found that
heartbreaking news was waiting for me. My dear sister
Elizabeth had been sold to a man who was taking her to
Natchez. Elizabeth had said she would rather die than go
to the Deep South, so her new owner had put her in jail
for safekeeping. I went to the jail the day I got back but
the jailer was away and I could not get in to see her.

I went home to my master in the country. The day

after I arrived, he came over to where I was working and started to talk to me very politely. I knew that something was wrong. After chatting for a while about my trips to New Orleans with Mr. Walker, he came to the point. He told me he needed money and that since he had sold my mother and all her children except me, it would be better to sell me than break up another of his slave families. He said I was used to city life and would probably prefer it to staying in the country anyway.

I had been listening with my head bowed but now I raised my head and looked him straight in the face. When I caught his eyes, he quickly looked down at the floor.

"Master, my mother used to tell me that you are a close relative. I have often heard you admit it yourself. And after you have hired me out and got, as I heard you say, nine hundred dollars for my services—after my bringing you so much money, are you going to sell me to be taken to New Orleans?"

"No, I do not plan to sell you to a Negro trader," he answered. "If I wanted to do that, I would have sold you to Mr. Walker. He offered a lot of money. But I would not sell you to a Negro trader. You may go into St. Louis and find yourself a good master."

"But I cannot find a good master in the whole city."

"Why not?"

"Because there are no good masters anywhere in Missouri," I said.

He was surprised.

"Don't you call me a good master?"

"If you were, you would not sell me," I replied.

"I will give you one week to find a master. You can surely do it in that amount of time."

The price set by my righteous master upon my soul and body was the insignificant sum of five hundred dollars. I tried to arrange to buy my freedom but he would not agree.

So I set out for St. Louis with the understanding that I would come back in a week with someone to become my new master. As soon as I got to the city, I went to the jail to try to see my sister but again I could not get in. Then I went to my mother, who told me Elizabeth's owner planned to start for Natchez in two days.

I went to the jail the next day and this time the keeper let me in. He knew it would be the last time I saw my sister. I cannot begin to describe that parting scene. I will never forget that day.

When I came into the cell, she was sitting all by herself in a corner. There were four other women in the cell, all belonging to the same man. He had bought them, he said, for his own use. Elizabeth was facing the doorway when I came through it, but she did not look up or show any sign of spirit until I stood right in front of her. Then she sprang up and threw her arms around my neck and wept. When she could speak, she told me to take mother and try to escape slavery.

60

"There is no hope for me," she said. "I must live and die a slave. But there is still hope for you."

Giving her as much good advice as I could, I took a ring from my finger and put it on hers and then said good-bye to her forever. I went back to my mother and then and there made up my mind to leave for Canada as soon as possible.

I had now been in St. Louis nearly two days. I was expected to be away from my master's farm only a week, so I thought I had better start the journey immediately. When I told my mother, I discovered that she was not willing to go with me. All her children were slaves, she said, and she did not want to leave them. She urged me to go, though—to make my way to freedom if I possibly could. But I would not accept the idea of her staying among these pirates when there was a chance of getting away from them. I finally persuaded her to agree to try to escape.

We decided to leave the next night. I had a little money with me, a few dollars I had earned from time to time running errands. I used it to buy some dried beef and crackers and cheese, which I brought back to her. She had found a bag to carry the food in.

Once in a while, I thought of my old master out in the country and how I was supposed to be finding a new master in the city. I waited nervously while the hours crept by.

At last it was time. My mother and I left St. Louis as

the clock struck nine. We traveled to the northern part of the city, where I had gone two or three times during the day, and found a skiff to take us across the river to Illinois. It was not my boat and I did not know who it belonged to. I did not care, either. It was fastened to the shore with a small pole which I loosened. After looking around and finding a board to use as an oar, I turned toward the city. Memories of my life in St. Louis ran through my mind. I said a long farewell to the place. Then with my mother settled in the skiff, I pushed off. The current was running very swiftly. I had not paddled into the middle of the stream before we were directly opposite the main part of the city and a short time later, we were at the Illinois shore.

I got my mother on land, leaped from the boat myself and turned it adrift. The last I saw, it was floating quickly down the river.

We took the main road to Alton and managed to pass through the town just at daybreak. Then we made for the woods where we stayed all day. We had to hide because we knew that Mr. Mansfield, the man who owned my mother, would start hunting for her as soon as he found out she was missing. Mansfield knew that I had been in the city looking for a new master and we thought he would probably go out to Dr. Young's farm to see if I had taken my mother to the country. Dr. Young might begin to wonder whether I had gone to Canada to find a buyer.

62

As soon as it was night again, we started on our gloomy way. We had no guide except the North Star which I had learned to recognize when I worked on the river. We continued to travel by night and hide in the woods by day. Each night, before we came out of our hiding place, we would look anxiously for our friend and guide, the North Star.

As we traveled north toward liberty, sometimes the heart in my body seemed to leap for joy. Other times I was so tired from walking I thought I could not go on. But I thought about slavery—the whips of the Democrats, the chains of the Republicans, the gospel of the blood-hounds and Christian slaveholders. When I thought about these things that all belonged to American democracy and religion and were now behind me, of freedom in front of me, I felt strong and forgot I was weary or hungry.

On our eighth night, we ran into a heavy rainstorm and, in an hour, we did not have a dry thread on our bodies. This made traveling harder. On the tenth day, we ran out of food and did not have the slightest idea how to get more. We finally decided to take a chance and stop at a farmhouse. No sooner said than done. We went up to a house and knocked on the door.

The people there treated us with kindness. Not only did they give us a hearty meal but also extra food to take along with us. They told us we should travel by day and rest by night, and even offered us shelter. Since we were now 150 miles from St. Louis, we decided it would be safe, so we stayed the night and did not go off until the next morning.

That day we went through thickly settled farm country and one small village. Although we were leaving a land of great suffering, our thoughts were often still there, with my dear sister and two beloved brothers. We were sad to be giving them up forever. But along with the sadness was the joy of knowing that when this journey ended, I would be free, I could call my body my own. I was just telling my mother how I was going to get a job in Canada and buy a little farm and earn enough money to buy my sister and brothers and how happy we would be in our own free home when three men rode up on horseback and ordered us to stop.

"What do you want?" I asked the one who seemed to be the leader.

The men got down from their horses and one of them took a handbill out of his pocket. It advertised us as runaways and offered a reward of two hundred dollars for finding us and delivering us in the city of St. Louis. The advertisement had been put out by Isaac Mansfield and John Young.

While they were reading the handbill out loud, my mother looked at me and burst into tears. A cold chill ran over me. It was a feeling I never had before and hope never to have again.

They took a rope and tied my hands and led us back

64

six miles to the house of the man who seemed the leader. It was about seven o'clock in the evening when we reached there. They gave us supper and separated us for the night. The two men stayed in the room with me all night.

Before the family went to bed, they gathered together for prayers. The man who had tied my hands with a strong rope just hours before read a chapter from the Bible and then prayed as though God approved of the act he had just committed on a panting fugitive slave.

The next morning a blacksmith came and put a pair of handcuffs on me, and we started our trip back to the land of whips, chains and Bibles. They did not tie up my mother but watched her very closely. We were taken back in a wagon. After four days we saw St. Louis. I cannot describe how I felt coming back to that city again.

As we rode across the river, Mr. Wiggins, who owned the ferry, asked me what I was doing in chains. He had not heard that I ran away. In a few minutes, we were in Missouri. As we were being taken directly to jail, several of my friends saw me and nodded in recognition as I passed. In the jail, my mother and I were locked into different cells.

While I was in jail, I heard that my master was sick and the news brought me joy. I prayed hard for him— not for his recovery but for his death. I knew he would be very annoyed to have to pay the men who caught me and, knowing how cruel he could be, I was afraid.

In jail I also heard that my sister, who had still been locked up when we left, had been taken south four days before we came back.

I had only been imprisoned a few hours when three slave traders came to look me over. They had already heard that I was in jail for running away and thought that my master would want to sell me. Mr. Mansfield, who owned my mother, showed up as soon as he was told she was back. He informed my mother that he would not whip her but he was going to sell her to a Negro trader or take her to New Orleans himself. My master left me in jail for a week, then sent a man to take me home. When I got there, the old man was well enough to sit up. He called me into his room.

"Where have you been?" he asked.

I said I had been following his orders. He had sent me to find a new master and I had been out looking for one.

"I did not tell you to go to Canada to find a master," he said.

I told him I had served him faithfully and through me he had been able to put hundreds of dollars in his pocket and I thought I had a right to my liberty.

"If I had not promised your father never to sell you for the New Orleans market, I would let a soul driver buy you tomorrow," he answered.

I was sent out to the fields where the overseer had orders to watch me carefully during the day and lock me up at night. The second day I was in the fields, I was flogged.

As soon as the master was well enough, he rode to the city and when he came back, he told me he had sold me to Samuel Willi, a tailor. I knew Mr. Willi. I had once been hired out to him for three or four months. His servants did not consider him a very bad man, but neither was he the best of masters. When I arrived at my new home, I found that my new mistress was very glad to see me.

Mr. Willi had two other slaves, Robert and Charlotte. Robert was a very good whitewasher and he hired himself out from his master—that is, he got his own jobs in the city, paid his master one dollar a day and took care of his own needs. In St. Louis, he was known as Bob Music. Charlotte was an old woman who did all the cooking and washing and cleaning in the house.

Mr. Willi was not a rich man and he felt he could not afford to keep many servants around him, so he decided to hire me out soon after I arrived. He knew I had worked on steamboats so he gave me the privilege of finding a job on the river. I promptly arranged to work for Captain J. B. Hill on the steamer *Otto* which sailed from St. Louis to Independence, Missouri. My old master, Dr. Young, did not tell Mr. Willi that I had run away; otherwise, Mr. Willi never would have let me go aboard a boat.

While I lived at Mr. Willi's house, waiting for the

Otto to sail, I faced a trial I was completely unprepared for. My mother, who had been in jail since our capture, was about to be taken to New Orleans to die on a cotton or rice or sugar plantation.

I had been to the jail several times but never was allowed to talk to her. I did find out, though, what boat she was sailing on and when it was leaving. I waited anxiously for that sailing date. At last the day came when I would see my mother for the first time since our separation and, for all I knew, the last time in this world.

I went aboard the ship about ten in the morning, and there she was, with some fifty or sixty other slaves. She was chained to another woman. When she saw me, she dropped her head but she did not make any other move. She did not cry. Her sorrow was too deep for tears. I ran to her, threw my arms around her neck, kissed her and, on my knees, begged her to forgive me. I was responsible for her fate; if I had not persuaded her to try to escape with me, she would not now be in chains in the hold of a boat going to the slave market of New Orleans.

Finally she raised her head and looked at me with the face of an angel.

"My dear son," she said. "You are not to blame for my being here. You did nothing more or less than your duty. Do not cry for me, I pray you. I cannot last long on a cotton plantation. I think my Heavenly Father will call me home soon—and then I will be free."

I could not bear any more. I thought my heart would

break inside my body. My mother saw Mr. Mansfield coming toward us and whispered in my ear:

"My child, we must part soon. We will not meet again on this side of the grave. You always said you would not die a slave, that you would be a free man. Now try to get your liberty. You will have no one to look after but yourself."

As she was whispering those last words, Mansfield came up to me.

"Damn you, leave here this instant. You made me lose one hundred dollars to get this wench back," he cried, kicking me at the same time with his heavy boot.

As I left, my mother shrieked, "God be with you!" Those were the last words I heard her say.

The love of freedom that had been burning in me just about went out. I felt ready to die. As the boat moved gently from the wharf and glided down the river, I realized my mother was indeed gone. After it was out of sight, I went home to Mr. Willi's house but I was so full of sorrow I hardly knew what I was doing half the time.

Finally the boat I was to work on was ready and I went on board. I preferred being on a boat to living in the city and stayed with the *Otto* until winter came and the sailing season was over. But it was not a pleasant experience. The captain was a drunken hard-hearted man who did not know how to handle himself or anybody else.

Eight

On our second trip, Mr. Walker, the Negro driver I had worked for, came aboard with about two hundred slaves, chained and handcuffed. Among them was a man who used to belong to the brother of my old master, Dr. Young. His name was Solomon. He was a preacher and belonged to the same church as his master. I was glad to see the old man. But the poor fellow! He wept like a child when he told me how he had been sold from his wife and children.

The boat carried five or six gangs of slaves during that

sailing season. The state of Missouri is very much in the business of raising slaves to supply the southern market. Men who breed slaves for the market can be found among all classes—from the richest official down to the lowest local politician who can scrape together enough money to buy a woman to use for raising stock, and from the Doctor of Divinity down to the humblest member of his church.

After the *Otto* put up for the winter, I lived at Mr. Willi's house and again began to make plans for my escape from slavery. The hunger to be free began to stir inside me again. Day and night, it would not let me rest. I thought about the northern cities I had heard of, and about Canada where many slaves I knew had found safety. Sleeping, I would dream I was free in Canada and when I woke in the morning, I would cry to realize I was still a slave in Missouri.

Mr. Willi treated me better than Dr. Young ever had but, instead of making me content, good treatment only made me unhappier because it helped me appreciate liberty more.

Mr. Willi was a man who liked money as much as most men do. Although he was not trying to sell me, he got an offer from Captain Price, a steamboat owner and merchant in St. Louis. Captain Price was willing to pay seven hundred dollars, which was two hundred dollars more than Mr. Willi had paid, and the profit was too good to resist. Captain Price wanted me for a carriage driver and Mrs. Price was very pleased with his bargain. The family included Captain and Mrs. Price and one child. They owned three servants besides me—one man and two women.

Mrs. Price was very proud of her slaves. She always kept them well-dressed and as soon as Captain Price bought me, she decided she needed a new carriage. Soon her husband bought one for her and they started preparing to have a turnout in grand style with me all dressed up as the driver.

One of the women servants was a girl about eighteen years old named Maria. Mrs. Price immediately tried to arrange a match between Maria and me. She would tell me that I should have a wife, that it would be so pleasant if I married a girl in the same family. But to get married while I was still a slave was the last thought in my mind. And even if I had wanted to marry, I would not have chosen Maria. After a short time, Mrs. Price accepted the fact that her matchmaking between Maria and me was a failure. She found out (or thought she found out) that I liked a girl named Eliza who was owned by Dr. Mills. She was so eager to get me a wife, she immediately tried to buy Eliza.

First, though, she thought it would be a good idea to talk to me a little about love, courtship and marriage. So one afternoon, she called me into her room and asked me to sit down. I did—but I thought that it was a little strange because servants are not very often invited to sit down with the master or mistress. She said that she realized I did not care for Maria enough to marry her.

I told her that was true.

"Isn't there a girl in the city that you love?" she asked.

Well, now, people do not generally like to tell their love stories to just anybody who happens to ask about them. This was certainly true of me. After a bit of flushing and getting my thoughts in order, I told her I did not want a wife.

"Do you not think something of Eliza?" she asked.

I said I did.

"If you want to marry Eliza, we will buy her if we can," she said.

I did not encourage this business. I was determined to try for freedom again and I knew that if I had a wife, I would not want to leave her behind and if I took her with me, our chances of success would not be very good. They bought Eliza anyway and brought her into the family.

The more I thought about the trap Mrs. Price was setting to make me happy in my new home, the more I was sure that I would not marry any woman on earth until I had my freedom. But that was my secret—and it put me in a very tricky spot. I had to keep on good terms with both Mrs. Price and Eliza. So I promised Mrs. Price I would marry Eliza but said that I was not quite ready. And I talked sweet to Eliza to keep Mrs.

Price from suspecting that I did not intend to get married.

I am speaking about marriage here, and it is very common for slaves to talk about it. Slaves marry—or at least they have wedding ceremonies performed. But there is no such thing as a legal marriage for slaves. A slave has never been tried for bigamy, for instance. The man can have as many women as he wants and the woman can have as many men. The law does not recognize these matings among slaves as marriages. In fact, some masters sell a woman's husband and then force her to marry another man.

Across the street from Captain Price lived a man named Farrar, a well-known doctor, who owned a married couple, Ben and Sally. One day he sold Ben to a soul driver and just a few days later, Sally married Peter, another man Dr. Farrar owned.

"Why did you marry Peter so soon after Ben was sold?" I asked her.

"Master made me do it," she said.

John Calvert, who lived up the street from our house, had a woman called Lavinia. She was quite young and was just about to be married when her man was sold and taken to St. Charles, twenty miles away. Mr. Calvert wanted to get her a husband but Lavinia refused to marry anyone else. Mr. Calvert whipped her so terribly that some of the local citizens had him arrested. The affair was hushed up. Nobody heard any more about it.

Lavinia did not die from that beating but Mr. Calvert almost did kill her.

Captain Price bought me in October, 1833. In December, the family sailed to New Orleans on a boat Captain Price owned. I was on board as one of the stewards. When we arrived in New Orleans, about the middle of the month, we took on some cargo for Cincinnati. The Captain decided to take his family on the trip north with him and, more interesting to me, I was to go with them. The long-awaited time to escape was near.

Captain Price was a little worried about taking me near a Free State or any place where it was likely that I could run away.

"Have you ever been in a Free State?" he asked me.

"Oh, yes," I said. "I have been in Ohio. My master took me there once, but I never liked a Free State."

He decided it would be safe to take me with them but to make double sure, they brought Eliza along.

"Do you think as much of Eliza as ever?" asked Mrs. Price. This was her way of testing me.

"Eliza is very dear to me, indeed," I said. "Nothing but death could part us. It is just as if we were married."

My speech had the result I wanted. The boat left New Orleans and started to sail north.

At different times, I had managed to earn little amounts of money which I saved for a rainy day. Now it was time to spend it! I bought some heavy cotton cloth and made a bag to carry food. I forgot about the miseries of the past. I was too busy thinking about my hopes for the future. The yearning to be free which had simmered low for a while burned bright. At night, when everybody was asleep and everything was peaceful and quiet, I walked around the docks planning my happy future.

I should have said that before I left St. Louis, I went to an old slave named Frank who was very well known among whites as well as slaves for being a fortuneteller. He was about seventy years old, over six feet tall and very thin. In fact, he was so skinny that his body did not seem strong enough to hold up his head.

Uncle Frank was a very great favorite with the young ladies, who went in great numbers to have their fortunes told. Everyone believed he could really read the future. Whether he could or not, everyone believed it and that is half the game.

I found Uncle Frank sitting in the chimney corner about ten o'clock one night. As soon as he saw me, the old man got up. I watched him as closely as I could in the dim light of the fire. He lit a lamp and held it up so he could look me full in the face.

"Well, my son, you have come to get uncle to tell your fortune, have you?"

"Yes," I said, but I did not know how he could tell the reason I came.

I gave him his fee of twenty-five cents and he began his fortunetelling by looking into a gourd filled with water. I do not know whether the old man was a seer himself or the son of a seer but I do know one thing: many things he told me came true. I do not believe in fortunetelling, but how could Uncle Frank see events in the future so correctly? Among the many things he told me, one was enough to repay me for the trouble I had finding him. He told me I would be free. He also said that I would have many trials on my way to freedom—and I thought, Any fool could tell me that!

Our first landing in a Free State was at Cairo, Illinois, a small village at the mouth of the Ohio River. We only stayed a few hours there. Then we went up the river to Louisville, Kentucky, where we unloaded some cargo. After that, we started to go north. Late on the night of December thirty-first, we tied up at a wharf at Cincinnati in the Free State of Ohio. The next day was January first, 1834, and I was twenty years old. I looked forward to New Year's Day as the beginning of a new era in my life. On that day I would leave slavery.

I did not close my eyes once during my last night. When I was not thinking of the future, I was remembering the past. I cried to think of my loving mother, my dear sister and brothers who were still alive. If I knew they were dead, I would have been less sad. In my mind I saw my mother in the cotton field, followed by a cruel overseer with a whip and no one to speak a comforting word to her. I saw my precious sister at the mercy of a Negro driver, forced to submit to his desire. No one who has not been a slave can imagine my agony.

Nine

At last it was morning and time to act. I realized that I could not take anything with me except what I was wearing—a half-worn suit of clothes. I stuffed what provisions I had in the pockets. Then while all the customary bustle was going on—the hands unloading the cargo, debarking passengers taking their baggage off the boat, oncoming passengers bringing their baggage aboard—I picked up a trunk as though I were helping out and went onshore into the crowd of people. I set the trunk down and made straight for the woods and there I stayed until night. I knew I could not travel during the day even in the Free State of Ohio without risking arrest. Early in my planning, I had made up my mind that I would not trust anyone, white or black. Not white because a slave is taught all his life that every white man is his enemy and an enemy to his race. And not black because twenty years as a slave taught me that even black men will be traitors. I had learned those lessons well while trying to escape with my mother.

After dark, I came out of the woods and followed a narrow path that took me to the main road. Once there, however, I did not know what direction to take. I could not tell north from south, east from west. The North Star which would have helped me lay hidden under clouds. I walked up and down the road for hours. Finally, around midnight, the clouds floated away and the North Star, the slave's friend, appeared in the sky.

As soon as I saw it, I knew my way and before daylight I had traveled northward twenty or twenty-five miles. It was the middle of the winter and very cold. My clothes were too thin. I was in pain from the weather. Fortunately, I had a tinderbox with me to make a fire of dry leaves and stubble when I needed one. Except for that, I surely would have frozen to death. Because I was not going anywhere near a house for shelter! I knew a man who belonged to General Ashly of St. Louis who had run away near Cincinnati, as I was doing. He was trying to reach Washington when he entered a house, was identified and caught and taken back into slavery. I felt that if anybody even saw me, I would suffer the same fate. I traveled only by night. I lay low during the day.

On the fourth day, my food ran out. That night I stopped at a barn by the road and took ten or twelve ears of corn I found there. The next day in the woods I roasted corn and feasted, thanking God for providing so well.

Feeling quite sure that my escape was successful and I would reach freedom, I began to think about the immediate future. What kind of work would I do? What name would I have?

As I said before in this book, my old master, Dr. Young, had no children of his own but took into his house a nephew, the son of his brother Benjamin. When the child arrived, his name like mine was William, and Dr. Young ordered my mother to change mine to something else. I was only around ten years old but even at that young age, I thought the way they changed my name so casually was a most cruel denial of my rights as a human being. I received severe floggings for telling people my name was William after orders had been given to change it. I had respect for my own name. But this was a battle I could not win while I was a slave. It was decided to call me Sanford and that was the name I was known by on my old master's farm and up to the time I escaped. I was sold to Mr. Willi under the name Sanford.

When I thought about what I would be called as a

free man, the first thing I decided was to take back my name William and forget the name Sanford which I hated, not because of the name itself but because it had been forced on me.

As for a last name, it is quite common in the South for slaves to take the name of their masters. Some slaves, of course, have a legitimate right to do exactly that. But I always detested the idea of being called by the name of either of my masters, Dr. Young and Mr. Willi. As to my father's name, I would rather be known as "Friday," the servant of some stray Robinson Crusoe, than to take his name for my own. So I was not only looking for liberty. I was also looking for a name. Not that the name had any importance compared to freedom—still, as I walked along the road, I kept saying, "William, William," out loud to get used to it before I came among people.

About the sixth day out, it rained hard and the rain froze into snow as fast as it fell. My clothes seemed covered with a sheet of ice. The wind blew the snow in my face. I was so cold I became numb. I could not go any farther. I managed to find some shelter in a barn but all night long I walked around inside that barn, clapping my hands to my arms to keep from freezing.

I look back at that snowy night as the crucial hours of my escape. Nothing but God's grace and that old barn kept me from freezing to death. As it was, I caught a fierce cold that settled in my lungs and stabbed me with every breath. My feet were so frostbitten that every step I took was painful. Sick, frozen, frostbitten, I went on for two more days and then I knew I had to find shelter or die.

Yet I was still less afraid of dying than I was of being caught and taken back to slavery. Nothing but the thought of freedom let me survive such trials.

Behind I left the whips and chains,
Before me were sweet Freedom's plains!

This, and this alone, cheered me on. Finally, to get relief from the terrible weather, I huddled behind some logs and brush and decided to wait there until somebody passed by. I hoped I would see some colored person, or, if not, someone who was not a slaveholder. I was sure I could spot a slaveholder as far as I could see him.

The first man who passed was riding in a buggy. He looked too high born for me to call to him. The next was a man on horseback. I tried to speak to him but I was so frightened I could not make a sound. After he went by, I left my hiding place and was walking toward the road when I saw an old man coming along leading a white horse. He wore a broad-brimmed hat and a very long coat and seemed to be walking just for the exercise. As soon as I saw him and noticed the way he was dressed, I said to myself, "You are the very man I'm looking for." And I was right.

As he came up to me, he asked me if I was a slave.

I looked at him for a while. Then I said, "Do you know anybody who would help me? I am sick."

He said he would help me, but asked me again if I was a slave.

"I am," I said.

He looked around him.

"This is a very proslavery neighborhood," he said. Then he told me to wait there, that he would go home and get a covered wagon for me.

I promised to wait. He got on his horse and soon was out of sight.

After he was gone, I wondered whether I should stay there. I worried that he had gone off to get someone to arrest me. Finally I decided to wait until he came back but to hide in such a way I could watch him as he approached. I waited an hour and a half, nervous every minute. Then he appeared with a two-horse covered wagon, the kind you see under the shed of a Quaker meeting house. The man turned out to be a Quaker.

He took me to his house but it took a lot of persuading to get me inside. I did not dare enter until his wife came out. Then I went gladly. I thought I saw something in the old lady's manner that told me even more than words that I was not only safe but welcome in her home.

However, I was not prepared for their hospitality. Their fault was that they were too kind. I never before had a white man treat me as an equal and the idea of a white lady waiting on me was even worse. The table was loaded with good food and I could not eat. If only they would let me sit in the kitchen, I thought, then I would be more than grateful.

When the old lady saw that my appetite failed me, she made me a cup of what she called "composition number six." It was so strong and so hot that I called it "number seven!" Soon I found myself completely comfortable with this kind couple.

At different times, when I have told this story, people have asked me how I felt being treated as a man by a white family, especially since I had just run away from one. I do not think I have ever been able to answer that question for during those moments, I was filled with one emotion that overwhelmed all the others: I was free.

The fact that I was now probably free rang like a bell in my ears. I think nobody in the world but a slave could appreciate the meaning of the words *free man* as deeply as I did those first hours. I wanted to see my mother and sister and tell them I was free. I wanted to see the slaves I knew in St. Louis and let them know I was free. I wanted to see Captain Price and say to him, "I am not your property any more. I am a man." I also wanted to inform Mrs. Price that she had to get herself another coachman. Most of all, though, I wanted to see Eliza.

Knowing that I was free—that I could walk, talk, eat and sleep like a man with no one standing over me with a bloody whip—made me feel as though I were somebody else and not myself at all.

Ten

The kind man who took me in was named Wells Brown. He was an abolitionist, a good friend to the slave. He was very old. His health was poor.

As I sat by the fire, my feet began to ache and I realized they were badly frozen. Then I became feverish. My Quaker friends helped me from the fire and got me to bed. They treated me as gently as though I were one of their own children. I stayed with them about two weeks. During that time, Mrs. Brown made me some clothes and the old gentleman bought me a pair of boots.

Their house was about fifty or sixty miles from Dayton, Ohio, and between one hundred and two hundred miles from Cleveland, on Lake Erie, which I had to cross to get to Canada. It will sound strange to foreigners but it is nevertheless true: I was an American citizen fleeing from a democratic Christian republic to find protection under the Queen of England. The people of the United States boast about their freedom but they keep three million of their own citizens in chains.

Before I left this good Quaker friend, he asked what the rest of my name was.

"I have no other name except William," I said.

"Well, thee must have another name. Since thee has got out of slavery, thee has become a man and men always have two names."

I told him that he was the first man to give me friendship and I would give him the privilege of naming me.

"If I name thee," he said, "I shall call thee Wells Brown after myself."

"But I am not willing to lose my name William," I said. "It was taken away from me by force once and I will not part with it again."

"Then I will call thee William Wells Brown."

"So be it," I said.

And I have been known as William Wells Brown ever since I left the house of my first white friend.

Wells Brown gave me some pocket money and once again I started off for Canada. I stayed on the road most of the time but about four days out, I went into a public house to get warm. As I was sitting in front of the fire, I heard the men in the barroom talking about some fugitive slaves who had just passed through the town. I was sure they were talking about me. I was afraid to move. I knew they would grab me the moment I got up. I finally worked up enough courage to rise and leave slowly and calmly. As soon as I was out of sight of the public house, I walked fast to the woods where I hid until dark. Then I walked all night and walked all the next day.

By this time, I had not eaten for two days and I was faint with hunger. The little cash my adopted father had given me bought me comfort but now it was all spent. The only thing I could do, I decided, was to go to a farmhouse and ask for food. At the first house I went to, a man came to the door and asked what I wanted.

"I would like something to eat," I said.

"Where are you from? Where are you going?"

"I have come some way," I said, "and I am on my way to Cleveland."

He hesitated for a moment or two. Then he told me he would not *give* me anything to eat, but if I would work there would be food.

I was upset that he refused to feed a starving man but I knew I could not spend time working there and I did not dare to tell him I was a runaway slave.

Just as I was turning away, his wife came up to the

door and asked the man what I wanted. He did not seem ready to tell her so she asked me. I said I had hoped for some food. She told me to come into the house and she would give me something to eat.

I turned back to the door but her husband blocked the entrance. She asked him to move and let me come in. He did not budge. She asked him again. She asked him two or three times. When he did not get out of the way, she simply pushed him to one side and bade me enter. I was never so glad to see a woman push a man around. Ever since then, I have been in favor of women's rights!

After serving me as much food as I could eat, the woman presented me with ten cents, which was all the money she had. She also gave me a note to a friend a few miles along the road. I thanked her with all my heart and pushed on my way.

At the end of three days, I arrived in the town of Cleveland, Ohio, on the banks of Lake Erie. It would be hard to imagine anyone in a more forlorn condition. I had had nothing to eat for the last forty-eight hours and traveling through woods and marshes and on icy roads had worn out my shoes and clothes so I looked bedraggled. Added to this was the fact that the lake was frozen over and no boats were running. All my hope of crossing to Canada came to an end. The only way to reach Canada now was to continue walking to Buffalo or Detroit and cross from one of those places by foot, but I was too weary to walk any farther. I decided to try to find lodging in Cleveland until the spring, when the boats would begin to run again.

I went from house to house until I found a man who offered me room and board if I would work for it. I sawed wood and did all the chores he asked me to in a welcome exchange for shelter from stormy winter weather such as I had never experienced before. So I survived my first weeks as a free man.

Soon afterwards, I found a job at the Mansion House, as a waiter. At first my pay here, too, was only my food. But in a few weeks the proprietor, E. M. Segur, hired me for twelve dollars a month. The first day he paid me twenty-five cents. This was not just the only money I had. It was the first money I received as a free man and it made me feel, indeed, that I was rich. What should I do with my twenty-five cents? I would not put it in a bank because, even if a banker would accept it, I would not trust him. I would not lend it to anyone because I was afraid I would not get it back. I carried the quarter in my pocket for several days. Finally I decided how to spend it. I paid fifteen cents for a spelling book. With the ten cents I bought some sticks of sugar candy.

You will say that fifteen cents for a spelling book was money well spent. I think the ten cents were well spent, too, for in the Segur household were two little boys who went to school every day and I wanted to turn them into teachers. I thought a little sugar candy would work like a charm on them.

The day I bought my book and candy, I went to saw in the woodhouse. A little after four o'clock, one of the boys passed by with his bag of schoolbooks.

"Johnny," I called to him, holding up the candy. "You see this?"

"Yes, give me a taste," said he.

"I have a spelling book, too," I said. I showed it to him. "Now, if you come to me in my room and teach me my ABC, I'll give you a whole stick of candy."

"All right," he said. "I will. But let me taste it now."

"No, I can't," I said.

"Let me have it now," he said.

I thought I had better give him a taste, until the right time came. I marked the candy stick about a quarter of an inch down and told him to bite that far and no farther. He made a grab, bit off half the stick and ran off laughing. I put the other half in my pocket and after a while, the other boy, David, came by with his bag of schoolbooks. I said nothing about the candy or my wish to get educated. I knew the other lad would communicate the news to him. In a short time, he returned, saying, "Bill, John says you have got some candy."

"Well," I said, "what of that?"

"He said you gave him some; give me a little taste."

"Well, if you come tonight and help me learn my letters, I'll give you a whole stick."

"Yes, but let me taste it."

"Ah, but you want to bite it," I said.

90

"No, I don't. Just let me touch my tongue against it."

I would not trust him as far as I had trusted John. So I called him to me and got his head under my arm and took him by the chin and told him to hold his tongue out. When he did, I drew the stick of candy very lightly across.

"That's very nice," he said. "Just draw it across my tongue again."

The night came on. The boys slipped out of their room and up to the attic where I slept and there they began teaching me the letters of the alphabet. We all lay on the floor covered with a blanket. First one would teach me a letter and then the other, and I would pass the sugar candy from one side to the other. I kept those boys on my ten cents' worth of candy for about three weeks. Before I left that place, I could spell and I could read.

Then I had to learn to write. You will understand that until this day I have never spent a minute in school, for I had no money to pay for schooling. I had to get my learning first from one, then from another.

I carried a piece of chalk in my pocket and whenever I met a boy, I would stop him and take out my chalk and get at a board fence and begin. I made some flourishes with no meaning and called a boy over and said, "Do you see that? Can you beat that writing?"

"That's not writing," said the boy. "Now what do you call that?"

What I wanted to do was learn to write my name.

"Is that not *William Wells Brown*?" I asked.

"Give me the chalk," he said, and he wrote out in large letters *William Wells Brown.*

I marked up the fence for nearly a quarter of a mile trying to copy until I could write my name. Then I went on with my chalking and, in fact, all board fences within half a mile of where I lived were marked over with some kind of figures I made trying to learn how to write.

Soon I bought an arithmetic book and a grammar and studied them equally hard. Next I bought other, general books and in leisure moments, I read them to improve my skills—and my knowledge. This reading of books whenever possible became my lifelong practice. Wherever I might be, there will always be with me a volume of grammar, mathematics, history or literature.

It was in Cleveland that I saw an antislavery newspaper for the first time. It was *The Genius of Universal Emancipation,* published by Benjamin Lundy. Although I had no permanent home, I subscribed to the paper. Now that I was out of slavery myself, it was my fervent desire to do what I could for the emancipation of my brothers still in chains. While a slave, I had regarded the whites as natural enemies of my race. It was, therefore, with no small pleasure that I learned about the existence of the salt of America—the abolitionists of the northern states, so despised in the South. I read with great care not only Mr. Lundy but also the great pioneer of the abolitionist cause, William Lloyd Garrison. After my own twenty years' experience of slavery, it is not surprising that I embraced Mr. Garrison's principles of "total and immediate emancipation" and "no union with slaveholders."

Eleven

When spring came, I took a job on a Lake Erie steamboat. I liked life aboard a steamer, which I knew from
my days as a slave, and I thought it would be relatively
safe; by working on a boat that ran from port to port, I
was in less danger of discovery and capture than if I re-
mained fixed in one locality.

1834 was a year of many happy changes in my life!
That summer, I met Miss Betsey Schooner, a free colored
woman, and became devoted to her so quickly that we
were married before the summer was over.

It is well known that many fugitives escape to Canada by way of Cleveland and although I chose not to do so, I found I could be of help to others. Sailing on Lake Erie, I regularly made arrangements to carry fugitives to Buffalo or Detroit. From these cities they could easily reach "the promised land" in an hour.

The friends of slaves, the abolitionists, knew I would transport the fugitives free of charge and they never failed to have a group waiting for me when the boat came back to Cleveland. I sometimes had four or five escaping slaves on board at one time. I did this for nine years. In 1842, I helped sixty-nine fugitives across Lake Erie and saw them safely on the soil of Canada.

Many of these escapes were interesting. One time, a fugitive had been hidden in the house of an abolitionist in Cleveland for ten days while his master was in town watching every steamboat that left the port. He had officers with him who were also on the watch; they guarded the house of the abolitionist every night. The slave was a young and valuable man, twenty-two years old and very black. His friends had just about given up hope of getting him away from his hiding place when they called me in. They asked what they could do.

"Is there a painter in the city who could paint the man white?" I asked. In an hour, following my directions, the black man was as white, and with as rosy pink cheeks, as any Anglo-Saxon. He was further disguised in a woman's dress with a thick veil over the face.

As the steamboat's bell rang for passengers to come aboard, a tall lady, dressed in deep mourning, leaning on the arm of an unusually tall man, could be seen going into the cabin of the steamer *North America*. The "lady" took her place with the other ladies. Soon the steamboat left the wharf. The slave catcher and his officers, who had been watching the boat since its arrival, were sure the slave had not escaped on the *North America* and went back to guard the house of the abolitionist. After the boat was well out of the port and on her way to Buffalo, I escorted the tall woman to her stateroom. The next morning, the fugitive, dressed in his slave's plantation clothes, said farewell to America, crossed the Niagara River at Buffalo and took up his new life in Canada.

I stayed on Lake Erie during the sailing season and, with Betsey and our two little daughters, lived in Buffalo during the winter. Buffalo was a place where many fugitives needed help to cross into Canada and I spent much of my time giving them help. My house in Buffalo could almost be called the "fugitive's house."

Niagara Falls was only twenty miles from Buffalo so slaveholders with one or two slave servants often went through the city on their way to see the famous waterfall. I was always on the lookout for such servants, to tell them that they were free by the law of the state of New York for New York had passed a state law which declared that on July 4, 1827, all slavery would end within her borders. I checked every colored servant I saw traveling with a white person and gave them whatever aid they needed.

My house also became the home of antislavery agents and lecturers on many other reform movements. For instance, as I took great interest in abolishing slavery, so did I take deep interest in the temperance cause, anti-drinking, because I found out that too much hard drinking was harming my black brothers. I felt that being sober and being educated were the two best ways to raise up the free colored people and to put them in a position where they could make a lie of the common feeling that a black man could not reach the level of white men. So, with others, I founded a temperance society among my brothers. Our efforts were very successful: in just three years, just in Buffalo, a society of almost five hundred people was formed from a population of seven hundred. I was elected president of the society three times.

Such activities, along with my intimate knowledge of the way the slave system worked, made the abolitionists feel that I was well qualified to arouse the attention of the people of the northern states to their cause.

In the autumn of 1843, I was invited by the Western New York Anti-Slavery Society to become a lecturer, and accepted the offer. Shortly afterwards, I began my work on behalf of my enslaved countrymen.

Mobs were very frequent in those days. Once, in 1844, I was scheduled to lecture in a church in Aurora, New York. The talk had been highly advertised and when I arrived, the church was surrounded by a howling set of men and boys, waiting to give me a warm welcome! I went in, opened the meeting and started my speech. But there was so much disturbance I had to stop. My friends and I did not know that in addition to the unsalable eggs which were being thrown around very freely, a bag of flour had been brought into the church, carried to the belfry directly over the entrance door and a scheme worked out. The flour was to be thrown over me when I left.

After I was driven from the pulpit by the rotten eggs, I stopped in the center aisle to discuss a single point with one of the respectable rowdies in the church. The audience became silent. I went on and spoke for more than an hour, with everyone giving me close attention. At the end, the lights were put out and the final preparations made to throw the flour over me—but I had evidently won over many of the mob. As we were jamming toward the door, one of them whispered:

"They are going to throw a bag of flour on you. When you hear someone say, 'Let it slide,' you look out!"

On guard—and knowing their signal—I planned a little fun at their expense. When some of the best-dressed and most respectable-looking people of the group, people with no sympathy toward my mission, filled up the doorway, I disguised my voice and called out, "Let it slide!"

Down came the contents of the bag, to the delight of

my friends and the confusion of the "enemy." The men at the door started quarreling. While they were settling their problems, my few friends and I quietly walked away unharmed.

I would like to be able to say that my success in my duties and responsibilities as a lecturer was matched by equal success in my family life. But I cannot.

My tours and meetings to arouse the attention of people to the great national sin of America kept me from my home for months at a time. Returning to the wife of whom I was so fond, and to sturdy little Clarissa and baby Josephine, was always a joy for me but I was soon to realize that my feelings were not shared by Betsey.

I have already mentioned that I had wed in haste. I must now add that I did not know my wife's family before we were married. Shortly afterwards, I learned that her mother was living with a second husband while her first husband was still alive; she had never been divorced. Then I found out that my wife's only sister was a mother without having become a wife. Still later, I discovered that her eldest brother, John, was in the Auburn, New York, state prison where he subsequently died. Although I had made a mistake in the family from which I had chosen a wife, I knew that one member of a family should not be blamed for the bad conduct of the others and I loved Betsey no less after I knew all these facts than I had before.

The beginning of the end of my marriage occurred in

December 1844, when I came home from one of my tours and Betsey treated me with anything but kindness. I was at home for months and constantly tried to find out why she had changed. But she would not tell me.

In March, I set out for a ten-day antislavery conference. I became sick and returned home four days before I was expected, at eleven o'clock at night. When I went into my house, I found Betsey and a friend of ours, Mr. James Garrett, in circumstances which I will not describe but which filled me with painful suspicions. They both tried to explain. They did not do it very well but since I had always thought of Garrett as one of my best friends and could not believe that my wife had acted as improperly as the situation suggested, I let the matter drop. The only thing I insisted was that Garrett not come to our house ever again.

But he did come again. At first Betsey denied it but then said he had been there to borrow my antislavery newspapers which previously, and with my permission, he took from my post-office box.

It is with great reluctance that I tell these things. One day, after a short absence, I happened to enter my house through the back door and found Garrett there under circumstances that were even more revolting than the first time. I knew beyond a shadow of a doubt that my worst fears were true. I decided to leave my wife, but her pleading, the helplessness of my children and my own unceasing attraction to this woman made me change my

100

mind. Instead I decided that we would leave Buffalo.

I chose Farmington, New York, a hundred miles away from Buffalo. In fact, I wanted to move there earlier and had even looked at a house to rent. Farmington was a center of antislavery activities and thus convenient for my work, but it also would be better for Clarissa and Josephine. In Buffalo, colored children were not allowed to go to school with the whites and I would not let my children go to colored schools because that would, in a way, seem as if I approved of the vile prejudice. In the village of Farmington, all children went to the same schools. At that earlier time, Betsey was so against the move that I gave up the idea. Now, however, she agreed.

But the new environment did very little to satisfy my wife. Within a year, she insisted on going back to Buffalo for a visit. She went alone but soon was writing me asking me to come to her; people were talking about her and only I could stop the gossip.

Against the advice of my friends, and my own judgment, I did go. I found her conduct had been so improper and was so widely known that, even while I tried to shield her, I was in a position that disgusted me. I left Buffalo alone and when she finally returned to Farmington, a separation was inevitable.

In the spring of 1847, we parted. She went west to Canada and from there to Detroit, where Garrett now lived. I went east, to New England. Four days after the final break, I set off with my two little girls to settle in

Boston and labor in the cause of the American Anti-Slavery Society as an agent of the Massachusetts Anti-Slavery Society. Putting the girls in school in New Bedford, I continued my mission.

Now I traveled even more, and many of my experiences on coaches and trains were insulting and created hardship because of my color, for even in the Free States the lot of the Negro was not the same as that of the whites. One time, I had traveled through Ohio, from Sandusky to Republic, on the railroad. At Sandusky, I learned that colored people were not permitted to take seats in cars with white people and that, because there was no Jim Crow car on the train, blacks generally had to ride in the baggage car. Nevertheless, I went into one of the best passenger cars, took a seat, crossed my legs and acted as though the car belonged to me. In a little while, a train conductor came by and asked what I was doing there.

"I'm going to Republic," I said.

"You can't ride here," said the conductor.

"Yes I can," I answered.

"No you can't."

"Why?" I asked.

"Because we don't allow niggers to ride with white people," was his reply.

"Well, I will stay here," I said.

"We'll see whether you will!" the conductor said, and left the car. By now other passengers were filling the seats. It was almost time for the train to start moving. Soon the conductor came back, accompanied by two strong-looking men. They took me by the collar and dragged me off. I had to keep my appointment, and the only way to do so was to take that train, so, just as the train started, I got into the freight car and seated myself on a flour barrel. I pulled out my abolitionist newspaper, *The Liberator,* and started to read. After the usual stops at other stations, the train was about four or five miles from Republic when the conductor came into the freight car and asked for my ticket.

"I have no ticket," I said.

"Well, then, I will take the money for the ticket."

"How much is it?" I asked.

"A dollar and a quarter."

"How much do you charge passengers in the passenger cars?"

"The same."

"And you think I will pay the same amount for riding in the freight car?"

"Certainly."

"Well, you're very much mistaken," I told him.

The conductor got very angry.

"Come on, black man. Out with your money and don't give me any of your nonsense."

I told him I would not pay the price he asked for. He wondered whether I intended to pay any fare.

"Yes, but not a dollar and a quarter," I told him. "I

will pay what's right. If I had ridden in the passenger car, I would pay you as much as others do. What do you charge for freight per hundred pounds on this railroad?"

"Twenty-five cents," said the conductor.

"Well, I have come on this train as freight and I will pay for myself as freight and nothing more. I will pay you thirty-seven and a half cents because I weigh exactly one hundred and fifty pounds."

The conductor took my thirty-seven and a half cents and left the car, saying that I was the most impudent black man ever to ride on that train.

Twelve

After lecturing in the antislavery cause for more than five years, I was invited by English abolitionists to visit Great Britain. At first I refused the invitation but I finally decided to go, for two reasons.

The first was a result of my increasing fame and good reputation as an agent and lecturer on behalf of my enslaved countrymen. In 1847, I had written a narrative of my life in slavery, which book was very well received and widely read. I was, therefore, well known as a fugitive slave. I did not have the rights of a citizen. By the

Constitution of the United States, I could be seized and sent back to slavery, no matter what Free State I was in. That my work took me constantly into places and situations where such an event was liable to occur at any minute was a fact I was aware of daily. There was a way I could remove myself from this danger. On January 10, 1848, Enoch Price, my last master, wrote an officer of the Anti-Slavery Society offering to sell me to him or other antislavery friends.

The letter ran:

Sir,

I received a pamphlet, or a narrative, so called on the title-page, of the Life of William Wells Brown, a fugitive slave purporting to have been written by himself. . . . This said Brown . . . is a slave belonging to me. . . . I do not want him as a slave, but I think that his friends, who sustain him and give him the right hand of friendship, or he himself, could afford to pay my agent in Boston three hundred and twenty-five dollars, so that he may go wherever he wishes to. Then he can visit St. Louis, or any other place he may wish. This amount is just half what I paid for him . . .

Such a purchase of freedom as Mr. Price suggested—and several of my friends wished to make—had been done for Frederick Douglass two years earlier. It freed him, as it would me, to serve the antislavery cause. But I would not accept it.

"I cannot accept of Mr. Price's offer to become a purchaser of my body and soul," I wrote the Society. "God made me as free as he did Enoch Price, and Mr. Price shall never receive a dollar from me or my friends with my consent."

The Society honored my decision but I had a new uneasiness at the knowledge that in the city of Boston was an unknown agent of the southern slaveholder.

But my personal safety in America was only one reason I decided to visit England. The second was that the Society felt it was a good idea always to have in England a Negro who would, by his very presence, give the lie to the doctrine of black inferiority. Many friends in England and America urged me to be such a person because they felt that no one could better plead the cause of those in bonds than one who had been bound with them.

So I made plans to set sail for foreign shores in the summer of 1849. When the American Peace Society heard I was going abroad, they elected me a delegate at the Peace Congress being held in Paris. They did not, however, pay any of the expenses of the trip. I went to Europe entirely at my own expense. I did not want to be a financial burden or make myself an unwelcome guest to anyone. I was taking with me the stereotype plates of my narrative. I hoped that by the printing and sale of the book, I would be able to meet any expenses that might arise beyond those that the hospitality of friends would cover.

Without my asking the favor, Mr. Garrison, President of the American Anti-Slavery Society, gave me several private letters to leading friends of freedom in Great Britain. I did not go out as an official representative of any antislavery society for I wanted to take full responsibility upon myself for whatever I might say or do.

Two evenings before I left, I was given a public hand of farewell at a large meeting of colored citizens in Boston. Resolutions were passed commending me to the confidence and hospitality of all lovers of liberty in America's motherland.

I sailed for England on July 18 aboard the steamship *Canada.* When the presence of a well-known fugitive slave on the ship became known, many of the passengers expressed interest in learning my history. I had a few copies of my narrative on hand, and it was sought after and read extensively. The narrative produced a considerable stir, especially among the passengers who were slave owners and proslavery.

In a few hours less than ten days after leaving Boston, the ship arrived at Liverpool. The anchor was cast and we were all tumbled, bag and baggage, at the door of the custom house. I waited nearly three hours before my name was called and, when it was, unlocked my trunks and gave them to the customs officer. His dirty hands did not improve the work of the laundress. He took one thing out and then another, and then he hauled out an iron collar which had been worn by a woman slave in Mississippi.

I had brought it with me to add visible support to my antislavery message. This instrument of torture became the center of attention; everybody turned around to look at it and ask questions about slavery. Some Americans standing by did not like the answers I gave but they did not say anything. The appearance of the collar ended the examination of my luggage. The customs officer must have been afraid that he would find something more hideous. He quickly put his mark on all my bags, passed them through and soon I was comfortably installed at Brown's Temperance Hotel, Clayton Square.

From Liverpool, I went to Dublin, Ireland, where I was warmly received by friends of the slave, men of esteem to whom I had letters of introduction from Mr. Garrison. I was publicly welcomed at a meeting of six hundred people, my first reception in the Old World. Her Britannic Majesty, Queen Victoria, was visiting her Irish subjects at the time so I had a chance of seeing Royalty in all its magnificence and regal splendor.

After twenty days in the Emerald Isle, I went to the Peace Congress in Paris, France. My reception was most flattering. In the presence of a large portion of the most distinguished people of Europe, many of whom had never seen a colored person before, I gave a brief talk about that war spirit of America which holds in bondage three million of my brothers. The short speech produced a deep response from my audience. When it was over, I was warmly greeted by the famous author, Victor Hugo, and the other distinguished men on the platform. At an evening party given by M. Alexis de Tocqueville, the French Minister for Foreign Affairs, and at other parties given for members of the Conference, I was received with marked attention. More than thirty of the distinguished English delegates to the Conference gave me invitations to visit their towns on my return to England and to lecture on American slavery.

When I went to England in 1849, it was not my intention to stay more than a year, but by the laws of the United States, I was the property of another man and the passage of the Fugitive Slave Act in 1850 increased by a hundredfold my belief, and that of my friends, that if I returned to America, I would immediately be arrested and sent back to slavery. This new Act was the legal encouragement of hunting and kidnaping slaves who had fled their bonds. Commissioners were set up to further the interests of slave hunters and severe penalties were provided to those who would obstruct the Act. Although the law stirred great excitement throughout the North, not only among the abolitionists but among all to whom personal liberty had become a rallying cry, its enforcement was too widespread for me now to be safe in any part of my country. I therefore decided to stay longer and to bring my motherless daughters to England so I could see to their education.

Yes, Clarissa and Josephine were now motherless, for the woman who could have had a home with my children, whose misconduct alienated me from her forever, died in January of the year 1851.

I wanted my daughters to receive an education that would qualify them to become teachers—an education they could not get in their native land. They arrived in Liverpool in July, 1851. They were, at the time, twelve and sixteen years old. Yet even this voyage was touched with persecution. The girls sailed on the Royal British mail steamer *America* under the charge of Reverend Charles Spear, a distinguished philanthropist who had become one of my friends. Even so, the company's Boston agent would not put them on the passenger list except under the heading of servants. The only reason they had to be called servants to come to England was because they were colored! The vile institution which had driven me into exile followed my children on board a ship flying the British flag. Soon after, I placed them in one of the best small girls' schools in France where they had no problem because of their color. The entire absence of prejudice against color in Europe is one of the clearest proofs that hatred of the colored person owes solely to the overpowering influence of slavery. After a year in France, my daughters attended the Home and Colonial School in London, the finest female educational college in Great Britain, numbering some two hundred students. There, as in France, they saw nothing to indicate the slightest feeling of ill will from other students because of their color.

Both trained to be teachers but were somewhat afraid that their color might be a barrier against their being hired as teachers. After completing their eighteen months in the training school, however, they were happily dis-appointed. Clarissa became mistress of a school in Essex, about forty miles from London, and, before she was fifteen years old, Josephine had a place at a school in London. Josephine had more than a hundred pupils and an assistant who was two years older than she. Needless to say, both her assistant and her pupils were white. It was not likely that she would be able to get a school of white pupils in America.

In early spring of 1851, William and Ellen Craft, two fugitive slaves, arrived in England to evade the Fugitive Slave Act. Being in a strange land without the means of support, they appealed to me just as I was about to make an antislavery tour through Scotland. I wrote at once for them to join me, for I knew them well. After their arrival at a certain house in Philadelphia on Christmas Day, 1848, they had committed themselves to my care while I was on a lecture tour of Pennsylvania. They had then appeared with me on more than a hundred lecture platforms throughout Connecticut and Massachusetts.

These two interesting fugitives were born into slavery in Georgia. William Craft, a tall black man, had been taught the trade of carpenter. Ellen, a house slave, was, like many southern slaves, as white as most Anglo-Saxons —thin-featured, straight-haired, and with hazel eyes, she

112

was a white slave whom no one on first seeing would suppose had a drop of African blood. With their owner's permission, they had been married, slave-fashion, and from the moment of their union, began arranging a plan to escape their house of bondage. Most of the plan was Ellen's idea. William, by hiring out, had managed over several years to save about one hundred and fifty dollars.

"Take part of your money and purchase me a good suit of gentleman's attire," Ellen said to him.

Their owners, like others who are called *good* slaveholders, were in the habit of giving their servants Christmas week as a time of rest and pleasure.

"When the white people give us our holiday," she continued, "let us go north. I am white enough to go as the master and you can pass as my servant."

"But you are not tall enough for a man," William said.

"Get me a pair of very high-heeled boots and they will bring me up more than an inch, and get me a very high hat, then I'll do," answered his wife.

"But then, my dear," said William, "you would make a very boyish-looking man with no whiskers or mustache."

"I could bind up my face in a handkerchief as if I were suffering dreadfully from the toothache and then no one would discover the lack of beard," said Ellen.

"What if you were called upon to write your name in the books at hotels, as I saw my master do when traveling, or were asked to receipt for anything?" William protested.

"I would also bind up my right hand and put it in a sling, and that would be an excuse itself for not writing."

"I fear you could not carry out the deception for so long a time, for it must be several hundred miles to the Free States," William said.

"Come, William, don't be a coward," she begged.

The day before Christmas, 1848, instead of going to the farm of Ellen's owner, as they said they were doing, they went to the railway station and took the six o'clock train for Philadelphia. Dressed in her new suit, her hat of the latest men's fashion, high-heeled boots, and with a pair of glasses on, she looked like a young college boy. Under the name of William Johnson, she took her seat in a first-class train while William, with his servant's ticket, went into the Jim Crow car. At Savannah, Georgia, they took a steamboat for Charleston and from there, by rail and steam, they arrived in Philadelphia in four days.

They had many thrilling adventures during their journey. At Charleston, "Mr. Johnson" stayed at the best hotel and was more than a little surprised to find himself sitting at the dinner table near Senator John C. Calhoun. The famous South Carolina Senator was the leading pro-slavery advocate in the government councils of Washington and throughout the South and the rest of the country. At both Richmond, Virginia, and Washington, D.C., they came close to discovery. The most amusing incident took place on the second day of the journey when "Mr. Johnson" made the acquaintance of a well-dressed old gentleman and his two daughters, both unmarried but of marriageable age, who were traveling to Richmond in the same railway car as "Mr. Johnson" and sitting near him. The old gentleman was rather talkative.

"You appear to be an invalid," he said, peering earnestly into the face of the young *man.*

"Yes, I have long been afflicted with inflammatory rheumatism," was the sad reply.

"Ah! I know what that is and can heartily sympathize with you," said the gray-haired gentleman.

Both father and daughters seemed to take great interest in the young invalid. William, acting the part of the servant, also attracted notice by his politeness and attention as he waited on his own "master" and the new acquaintances.

"That is a valuable servant of yours," said the old gentleman.

"Yes, sir," said "Mr. Johnson," "he is a boy I am very much attached to."

When the travelers approached Richmond, it was discovered that Miss Henrietta, the older of the young ladies, seemed to have more interest in the young man than one would entertain for a passing acquaintance.

"I'm sure you must be tired," said the old gentleman. "Why don't you stop with us and rest yourself for a few days? My wife, knowing you have been our traveling companion, will be glad to welcome you and my daughter, Henrietta here, will be delighted."

Miss Henrietta, feeling that this gave her an opportunity to speak, said, "Do, Mr. Johnson, stop and regain your strength. We have some pretty walks about Richmond and I shall be pleased to show them to you."

The young invalid found that this was carrying the joke too far. He gave, as an excuse for declining the invitation, that urgent business demanded his immediate presence in Philadelphia and promised them he would pay them a visit upon his return. The fugitives then sped to Philadelphia.

For several months, William and Ellen Craft traveled in company with me in England as they had done in New England, telling their story simply and making my own denunciation of slavery even more effective. Afterwards, they were able to satisfy their thirst for education by gaining admission to Lady Byron's School in Surrey where they studied for two years.

In May, 1851, a party of antislavery friends invited me and William and Ellen Craft to the Great Exhibition in London, which had exhibits and was attracting visitors from countries all over the world. The honorable way we were received by distinguished people who knew of us and our history, and the freedom with which we walked through the American section, was a rebuke to the many Americans present. It showed them the great sin of their country—slavery—and its great folly—prejudice of color.

A curious thing happened during the Exhibition. Among the large number of American visitors was my late master, Enoch Price, who made diligent inquiries about his lost piece of property—not, of course, with any view to reclaiming me. To my regret and the regret of Mr. Price, he was without success. It is satisfying to say that the master spoke highly of me and expressed a wish for my future prosperity. This fact tends to prove that prejudice of color is to a very great extent a thing of place and association. However, if Mr. Price had left behind letters of manumission for me, letters that set me free so I could, if I wanted to, return to my native land, he would have given a more practical proof of his respect and the sincerity of his desire for my welfare.

Thirteen

In 1852, I found that because of the shortness of the lecture season, which in England lasts only from November to May, and its providing an uncertain living, I must find another way to support myself and my daughters. Accordingly, I began to write articles for the British press. Having no education except what I had acquired by reading as much as I could, I often had to rewrite my articles. Most of what I wrote was on American subjects —Daniel Webster, the death of Henry Clay and other topics. These were received gladly by the London newspapers and I was liberally paid, although many times after the evening mail brought me newspapers and letters from America, I would write all night to have an article ready for a morning newspaper.

In the autumn of 1852, I published a book, *Three Years in Europe*, which consisted principally of twenty-three letters I had sent to abolitionist newspapers and personal friends in America. Devoted to places I had seen, people I had met and meetings in which I had participated during my years in England, the book received much attention. It brought me prominently before the public and gave me a position among literary men which was never before enjoyed by a colored American. It did much for antislavery feelings in England. One London newspaper, the *Morning Advertiser,* said in its review: "The impressions of a self-educated son of slavery, here set forth, must hasten the period when the senseless and impious denial of common claims to a common humanity, on the score of color, shall be scouted with scorn in every civilized and Christian country."

The *London Literary Gazette* said: "The appearance of this book is too remarkable a literary event to pass without notice."

By 1853, I was doing very well. My lectures were well attended and my book was selling extensively. In addition to my own endeavors, there was an extra reason for this success. *Uncle Tom's Cabin* by Mrs. Harriet Beecher Stowe, published the year before, had created a deep interest in American slavery on the part of the English. An anniversary meeting of the British and Foreign Anti-Slavery Society in London in May 1853 gave ample proof of this fact. Mrs. Stowe was a guest of honor and her husband was a speaker. No meeting during the year caused so much talk and excitement.

Uncle Tom's Cabin had come down upon the dark abodes of slavery like a morning's sunlight, unfolding for all eyes the enormities of "the peculiar institution" and awakening sympathy in hearts that had never had compassion for the slave before. If Exeter Hall, where the meeting took place, could have held fifty thousand people instead of five thousand, it would still have been filled to capacity. All available tickets had been sold more than a week before the event came off and every day hundreds more applied for tickets. For those who might be called Mrs. Stowe's converts, that lady was the center of attention. The older abolitionists came for the cause.

I entered the great hall an hour early and found the place filled. There was hardly any standing room, except on the platform which officials were keeping clear. At half-past six, the Earl of Shaftesbury appeared upon the platform, followed by the committee and speakers. There was the most deafening applause. The noble Earl, who has many more noble qualities than that of a mere nobleman, made the opening speech, and a good one. While he was speaking, Her Grace, the Duchess of

Sutherland, came in and took her seat in the balcony at the right of the platform. A half hour later, a greater lady (the authoress of *Uncle Tom's Cabin*) made her appearance and took her seat next to the Duchess.

At this point in the meeting, there was a fervor in the hall that can better be imagined than described. The waving of hats and handkerchiefs, clapping of hands, stamping of feet, and screaming and fainting of ladies went on as if it were part of the program. Meanwhile, thieves were at work helping themselves to the contents of pockets where the crowd was thickest. The police made a few arrests which encouraged the pickpockets to leave.

As soon as order was restored, the speaking went on. Professor Stowe, as might be expected, was looked upon as the lion of the speakers since he was both clergyman and husband of the great guest of honor. But his talk disappointed everybody—except those of us who knew enough about American men of the cloth not to expect much from them on the subject of slavery. Professor Stowe was not very young, but he was a child in the antislavery movement. He was lisping his ABC's, and if his wife succeeded in making him a good scholar, she found it no easy thing.

In the autumn of that year, 1853, I was still going the rounds, giving lectures on American slavery, and sometimes on other subjects, such as temperance, to technical and literary institutions and was looking over, as well, the proof sheets of a novel which I called *Clotel; or the President's Daughter.*

This new work of mine, then going through the printing press, was a book of nearly three hundred pages about slave life in the southern states. I have always felt that Englishmen should feel a lively interest in the abolition of slavery, for slavery had come into the American colonies while they were still controlled by the government of Britain. If I could add anything new to the information already given to the English public through other, similar publications, and could thus help bring British influence to bear on abolishing American slavery, the purpose of the novel would have been accomplished.

Clotel, like my earlier book written and published in England, helped me slowly work my way up in English literary society.

Few Americans visiting England have ever had better opportunity to see the conditions of all classes of society than I. Writing and lecturing, I saw every phase of life in England, Ireland, Scotland and Wales. I enjoyed the hospitality of the lord in his magnificent country estate and the peasant in his lowly cottage. But, even though I mingled with some of the best men and women of Europe, I never forgot my countrymen in bonds or overlooked the fact that I myself was closely connected with them. I kept track of every proslavery man who came to England to speak for slavery, staying at his heels wherever he went and exposing him and holding him up to the scorn and contempt of the people of Great Britain through the columns of the English newspapers. Every first of August of my last three years in England, I held a large meeting of fugitive slaves for the purpose of laying their wrongs before the British nation and, at the same time, giving thanks to God for their present liberty. The speeches made by the fugitive slaves were highly impressive and the halls, usually filled to overcrowding, resounded with deafening applause as the most noted English abolitionists made their appearance and took their seats on the platform. At one meeting could be seen near the door the greatest critic of the age and England's best living poet. Thomas Macaulay, the critic and historian, had laid down his pen and entered the hall, while near him stood the newly appointed Poet Laureate of England, Alfred Lord Tennyson. The aristocratic poet had been swept in by the crowd and was standing with his arms folded, beholding for the first time, and possibly the last, so large a number of colored men in one room. The gathering was most spirited and a good impression was made upon the assembled crowd.

In the spring of 1854, a few ladies in England, generous in their sympathy and liberal in their philanthropy, wanted to give me the right to return to the United States by purchasing my freedom. After almost five years away, I wished to return to the land of my birth. I watched with interest the doings of my old co-workers as I read of meetings and conferences in the pages of the

Liberator and the *Standard*. I never took up a copy of
those American abolitionist newspapers without feeling
like taking the next boat for Boston. I was not tired of
Old England but I wanted to be back in America.

But I did not want to go back as a hidden spectator.
I wanted to be a soldier in the moral war against the
cruel system of oppression that kept three million of my
countrymen groaning in the prison house of slavery. Pro-
pelled by these feelings, I agreed to the request of my
friends. They communicated with my old master to buy
my freedom and, after a time, the deed was accomplished.

This is how an American disposes of his neighbor by
the bill of sale called a Deed of Emancipation:

"*Know all men by these presents*, That I, Enoch Price,
of the city and county of St. Louis, and State of Missouri,
for and in consideration of the sum of three hundred dollars, to be paid to Joseph Greely, my agent in Boston,
Mass., by Miss Ellen Richardson, or her agent, on the
delivery of this paper, do emancipate, set free, and liberate
from slavery, a mulatto man named Sanford Higgins, *alias*
Wm. Wells Brown, that I purchased of Samuel Willi on the
2d October, 1833. Said Brown is now in the fortieth year
of his age, and I do acknowledge that no other person holds
any claim on him as a slave but myself.

"In witness whereof, I hereunto set my hand and seal,
this 24th day of April, 1854.

"ENOCH PRICE.

"Witness, { OLIVER HARRIS,
JOHN A. HASSON."

"STATE OF MISSOURI, COUNTY OF ST. LOUIS, s. s.
"In the St. Louis Circuit Court,
April Term, 1854.   April 25th.

"Be it remembered, that on this 25th day of April, eighteen hundred and fifty-four, in the open Court, came Enoch Price, who is personally known to the Court to be the same person whose name is subscribed to the foregoing instrument of writing as a party thereto, and he acknowledged the same to be his act and deed, for the purposes therein mentioned;—which said acknowledgment is entered on the record of the Court of that day.

"In testimony whereof, I hereto set my hand and affix the seal of said Court, at office in the city of St. Louis, the day and year last aforesaid.
"WM. J. HAMMOND, *Clerk.*"

"STATE OF MISSOURI, COUNTY OF ST. LOUIS, s. s.

"I, Wm. J. Hammond, Clerk of the Circuit Court in and for the county aforesaid, certify the foregoing to be a true and correct copy of the Deed of Emancipation from Enoch Price to Sanford Higgins, (*alias* Wm. Wells Brown,) as fully as the same remains in my office.

"In testimony whereof, I hereto set my hand and affix the seal of said Court, at office in the city of St. Louis, this 25th day of April, eighteen hundred and fifty-four.
"WM. J. HAMMOND, *Clerk.*"

125

"STATE OF MISSOURI, COUNTY OF ST. LOUIS, S. S.

"I, Alexander Hamilton, sole Judge of the Circuit Court within and for the Eighth Judicial Circuit of the State of Missouri, (composed of the County of St. Louis,) certify that William J. Hammond, whose name is subscribed to the foregoing certificate, was on the date thereof, and now is, Clerk of the Circuit Court within and for the County of St. Louis, duly elected and qualified; that his said certificate is in due form of law, and that full faith and credit are and should be given to all such his official acts.

"Given under my hand, at the city of St. Louis, this 26th day of April, eighteen hundred and fifty-four.

"A. HAMILTON, *Judge.*"

"July 7th, 1854. I have received this day Wm. I. Bowditch's check on the Globe Bank for three hundred dollars, in full for the consideration of the foregoing instrument of emancipation.

"JOSEPH GREELY,
"BY THOMAS PAGE'S authority."

I was now free to return to my native land to battle the institution which withers and curses the land, which blasts everything that it touches, which lies a heavy weight on the breast of the nation, which casts a shadow over the genius of the American Revolution and which makes our "democratic" country the scorn and byword of the inhabitants of European countries ruled by kings.

126

Fourteen

What a change five years make in one's life. The summer of 1849 found me a stranger in a foreign land, where I was completely unknown and the laws and customs and history of the country were a blank to me. But how different the autumn of 1854. I had become so familiar with England that I had begun to imagine that I was an Englishman, by habit if not by birth. The British people had endeared themselves to me by making me feel at home wherever I went. It was with a palpitating heart that I bade farewell to them, country and people, as I set sail on the *City of Manchester* on September 6 for my native land.

My native land! Within a few hours after the ship docked in Philadelphia, I knew what treatment I had to expect from my fellow countrymen. I was in the company of two foreigners, fellow passengers from England. We had ridden on the same train from London to Liverpool. We had stayed at the same hotel at that city. We had crossed the Atlantic enjoying the same privileges throughout the voyage. They had toasted their arrival in the land of liberty.

Now we walked up the streets of Philadelphia together and hailed an omnibus going in our direction. It stopped and the two foreigners got in and were given seats. I, the American born, whose grandfather had fought in the American Revolution, could not enter.

"We don't allow niggers to ride in here," I was told.

I had returned a free man by the act of British philanthropists but I scarcely felt more free than I did twenty years earlier when I was working as the servant of Enoch Price. I had felt then that I had as good a right to my freedom as the man who said I was his property. That was why I had left and come to the North. I asked myself, as I had done so often while I was in Europe, why I could stop at the best hotels in London or Paris or Rotterdam but not in Philadelphia; ride on a coach or omnibus or rail car or steamboat in Great Britain or on the continent but not here. It was not because of the color of my skin. It was because of the influence of slavery.

I thought of my daughters, who were kept out of school in the state of New York and would have grown up ignorant if they had stayed in America. Away from this country, they were received and treated according to their merits. At that moment, Clarissa was teaching Anglo-Saxons at a school in London, while Josephine was continuing her studies in France in order to further progress in the same profession.

I would never cease to remind Americans, who boasted of their freedom and Christianity, to do their duty to their fellow men.

Upon my arrival in Boston, which would again be my home ground, the abolitionists welcomed me at a large public meeting. The speakers were William Lloyd Garrison, William C. Nell and Wendell Phillips, the three outstanding figures of the antislavery movement.

Mr. Garrison paid me warm tribute.

In Mr. Nell's speech, he made a pun about my newly purchased freedom from my former owner.

"Let us thank God," he said. "You are now beyond *Price*."

Mr. Phillips spoke most eloquently of my coming "home to no liberty but the liberty of suffering—to struggle in fetters for the welfare of his race."

I was glad to see the smiles of my old associates and receive the approval of my course by my fellow colored citizens.

During the next years, I continued writing, and traveled the length and breadth of the Free States, lecturing at meetings large and small. Slavery was my deepest concern but I worked for other causes as well, for temperance as I had done since my early days in Buffalo, women's rights and, especially, the rights of the free colored person. In traveling through the country, I faced the prejudice that meets the colored man at every step.

In the autumn of 1854, I prepared an American edition of my book, *Three Years in Europe.* It was called *The American Fugitive in Europe. Sketches of Places and People Aboard.* I am happy to say it had a rapid sale.

By 1857, I had turned toward writing plays. This was for my own amusement and not with the remotest thought that they would ever be seen by the public eye. However, I read one, *The Escape; or, A Leap for Freedom,* privately to a circle of my friends and through them was invited to read it before a literary society. Soon I was giving dramatic readings as well as lectures in the halls. Some people would pay to hear a drama who would not give a cent to an antislavery meeting. At Hartfort, Ohio, once, after three lectures we took up ninety-five cents. Three days later, I read a drama at the same place, charged ten cents at the door, paid two dollars to rent the hall and ended with five dollars after all expenses. This was more than the lectures, Mrs. Lucy Newhall Colman, Mr. Joseph Howland, and myself, had taken up in collections the previous ten days.

In 1859, in Boston, I gave what a reporter for one of the abolitionist newspapers called "an entertaining and instructive dissertation on Love, Courtship and Marriage." This particular topic was not so far from the mark as my earlier marital history might suggest, for I had then been courting for more than a year Miss Annie Elizabeth Gray, the daughter of Mr. and Mrs. William H. Gray of Cambridgeport, Massachusetts. On April 12 of the following year, Miss Gray became my wife. My bride was twenty-five years of age. I was forty-five. More I need not say than that she has been my true companion and helpmeet from that day.

The year 1859 will be long remembered for the bold attempt of John Brown and his companions to burst the locked door of the southern house of bondage. On Sunday night, October 16, John Brown, with twenty followers, five of them colored, captured the town of Harper's Ferry in the state of Virginia in a premature effort to free the slaves. It is true that the little band of heroes dashed themselves to death. Those who were not killed at the scene were later captured and hung. But they shook the walls of the prison from top to bottom and frightened every tyrant in the South.

It was then increasingly important to create an active public opinion against slavery. In Massachusetts, I had heard a Boston audience receive a speech by Senator Robert Augustus Toombs of Georgia, an archdefender of slavery, not with the silence I had expected, not with hisses, but with applause. And that was before John Brown's martyrdom.

Toward the close of 1860, when the government, in the hands of President Buchanan, was little more than a tool for those who were getting ready to take the southern states out of the Union, the spirit of compromise on the part of the North toward the South and its institution of slavery was apparent on all sides. It showed itself in such unmistakable terms that friends of freedom were seriously concerned for the future of American liberty. From the nomination of Abraham Lincoln for the Presidency to his inauguration, mob law ruled in many of the cities and large villages. But the mobs achieved little. In the South, the people would listen to no conciliatory proposals, and six weeks after Mr. Lincoln was in Washington, the southern states withdrew from the United States.

The fall of Fort Sumter seemed to many to be the start of a new era for the black man, and when Mr. Lincoln called for 75,000 volunteers to put down the southern rebellion, a large public meeting of colored men was held in Boston at which the audience offered many patriotic sentiments. It was thought that victory by the Union would end slavery. The meeting resolved that colored men would raise an army of 50,000 to defend the Union if they were permitted to enlist. Colored women would go as nurses, seamstresses and warriors, if need be, to crush the rebellion. I protested the resolution, saying that the government in Washington had given no sign it would do anything about ending slavery. This was an unpopular view in the general excitement of the times but I felt that my many years of labor on behalf of the slaves earned me the right to speak freely as well as frankly. I thought that the self-respect of my black brothers should keep them from begging the government for the chance to defend it. For these views, I was denounced as a slaveholder by one venerable gentleman at the meeting and as a liar by another.

The old work of bringing the right and wrong of slavery before the hearts and consciences of men needed to be done now as much as ever before. Slavery had received a severe blow but the war was begun with the purpose of restoring the nation as it was and that could mean leaving the black man where he was.

By 1862, I was deep in a new work of writing that I, and my friends in Boston, thought was just the book needed at that hour to place the Negro in a right position before the country. This was *The Black Man: His Antecedents, His Genius, and His Achievements*, a volume of three parts. One was a brief memoir of myself, another was a history of the black race in ancient times and the third consisted of fifty-three biographies of well-known persons of color. The purpose of the book was to meet and disprove the arguments of those who talked of the "natural inferiority" of the blacks. It was also intended to fill in a lack, long felt among our abolitionist group, of a work containing sketches of people who, by their own genius, ability and intellectual development, had overcome the many obstacles that slavery and prejudice threw in their way, and raised themselves to positions of honor and influence. When this book was published in 1863, it received much attention.

On January 1, 1863, I participated in an all-day celebration of the Emancipation Proclamation and predicted that it would ultimately result in emancipation for slaves in every state, not only those states in rebellion. This longed-for day came to pass in January two years later, with the House of Representatives passing the Thirteenth Amendment to the Constitution. On April 9, scarcely four months afterwards, General Lee with his whole army surrendered to General Grant and the Southern Confederacy fell. The night of slavery with all its foul and pestilent horrors was gone. The dawn of freedom had come.

The time has now arrived to bring these pages to a close. My twenty-two-year career as an antislavery lecturer and agent is over but I shall still work on behalf of the black man in lectures and speeches and in writing history books which show him in his human and successful light. I shall urge my brothers to self-elevation—to the desire to educate our children, give them trades or professions and let them acquire the assets within themselves that will give them wealth and influence. During the Rebellion and at its close, the question of Negro equality overshadowed all others and to this question I must continue to address myself. It is the duty of the nation, having once clothed the colored man with the rights of citizenship and promised him in the Constitution full protection for those rights, to keep this promise most sacredly.

William Wells Brown, reformer and author of the first travel book, the first novel, the first play and the first histories written by a Black American, died in Chelsea, Massachusetts, in November 1884, at the age of sixty-nine.

The Major Works
of William Wells Brown

The major works of William Wells Brown

Narrative of William W. Brown, A Fugitive Slave (1847;
    revised 1848, 1849)

*Three Years in Europe: or, Places I Have Seen and People
    I Have Met* (London, 1852; enlarged and reprinted
    in 1855 as *The American Fugitive in Europe*)

*Clotel; or the President's Daughter, a Narrative of Slave
    Life in the United States* (London, 1853; revised
    and reprinted under different names in 1860–61,
    1864 and 1867)

The Escape; or, A Leap for Freedom (*A Drama in Five
    Acts*) (1858)

*The Black Man: His Antecedents, His Genius, and His
    Achievements* (1863)

*The Negro in the American Rebellion; His Heroism and
    His Fidelity* (1867)

*The Rising Son; or, The Antecedents and the Advance-
    ment of the Colored Race* (1874)

My Southern Home: or, The South and Its People (1880)

136